PRIZE MONEY

by

Adam Hardy

THUNDERCHILD PUBLISHING
Huntsville, Alabama

This is a work of fiction. All of the characters, organizations, and events portrayed in this novel are either products of the author's imagination or are used fictitiously.

PRIZE MONEY

ISBN-13: 978-1523750597
ISBN-10: 1523750596

Published by Thunderchild Publishing
1898 Shellbrook Drive
Huntsville, AL 35806

Cover design by Dan Thompson

Table of Contents

Chapter One

Lieutenant George Abercrombie Fox of His Britannic Majesty's ninety-eight-gun ship of the line *Tiger* swore luridly and hauled to a halt before the wardroom door, turned around and ran off to his station on the lower gun deck. All over the three decker the boatswains mates' pipes were twittering and the marines' drums rolled their hollow echoes; the slap of horny feet on the decks, the ordered tramp of the marine's boots, the crash and rumble as the guns were cleared away, the heavy rush of human bodies flying to their quarters, all this bustle showed an instant response to the order: "Beat to Quarters! Clear for Action!"

The door of the wardroom he had nearly reached looking for a place of comparative quiet to read his letters again, the very bulkhead itself in which the door was set, would be torn down by now and be well on its way to being stored below. The marine sentry would be doubling to his post. All the galley fires would be doused. Boys were busy sprinkling sand over the decks. Fox cursed again and roared into the area around the mainmast. If this battery was the last in coming to readiness he'd be tongue-lashed, if not worse, by the first lieutenant, Mr. Paunceford, and his men, knowing this, were all the more ready to jump when Fox cursed and drove them.

A couple of months of blockade duty aboard *Tiger* had taught him that any strange sail might be the enemy but was more likely to be a British despatch vessel or a stray from a convoy; the French weren't coming out, that was what Fox thought and the conviction irked him as it irked every officer and man aboard the Channel Fleet. The sail that had caused this hullabaloo must be French — Vice-Admiral Sir Blundesely Creighton and Captain Sir John Pulteney might be a pair of antiquated fossils in Fox's estimation; but they weren't fools enough to clear away for action a ninety-eight three decker over a sail whose identity they had not ascertained.

Even then — even then the enemy must have more power than a mere lugger or brig. They could deal with that kind of force without clearing for action; just putting out the galley fires would suffice.

Fox began to brighten up. Maybe, just maybe, Monsieur Jean Crapaud was coming out. Maybe the battle for which the whole Channel Fleet longed with a fervour that monotonous blockade-duty could never dull was on him at last.

In the bustle of casting off the guns' lashings, of the captains of the guns fitting their locks and trigger lanyards collected from the gunner's mates, their priming powder horns slung around their necks, the clash and clatter as worms, sponges, rammers, were laid ready to hand, the splash of water as the pumps wet the deck, the drinking tubs were filled from the scuttle-butts and the sea water tubs were filled ready to wet the sponges, a burst of obscenity and a sliding smash and crash made Fox whip around. A whole raffle of gear lay across the deck and some filthy sticky mess trickled across the deck — his deck. A scared-looking ship's boy lay in the mess, his water-bucket, overturned. Fox looked at the lad as he scrambled up, tousled-haired, scared, the corners of his mouth drawing down. His hands shook.

Beneath the low curve of the deck beams with their becketted and hanging freight of stores and tools, the battle-lanterns cast a livid blue light upon the scene. From the nearest thirty-two pounders the men all stared at Fox, waiting, their eyes like fireflies, their mahogany-brown faces turned towards him devouring him with their silent contempt.

Fox had need of making the barest minimum of stoops beneath the deckbeams that made a six-foot man crouch. He looked at the boy and at the filthy deck.

"You — Affleck, Larber — help clear that away. The lad couldn't have knocked it all over by himself." Fox stood like some Old Testament judge graven in granite as the men jumped to obey. "Run and fill your bucket again, lad. Remember, run and do your duty. That's all you have to worry about."

As the powder monkey scampered off Fox said: "Now, you lubbers, get that deck swabbed off. Sprinkle more sand." He lowered his eyebrows and glared at Mr. Midshipman Doyle who that moment panted up, swallowing something he had been chewing. Doyle was in command of the six guns in this division.

"Mr. Doyle, get this pig-sty cleaned up; keep these merry bastards at it."

Without waiting for the reply — it could only be the conventional: "Aye, aye, sir!" Fox stalked aft. He was responsible for the larboard side battery of fifteen thirty-two pounders on the lowest gun-deck of the ship. He had Doyle to command six of those guns, and two gunners' mates to command the balance. In France the revolution was convulsing along, the Terror, so it was claimed, had ended and this new Directory was falling into bankruptcy. The little Corsican general had done great things in Italy — Buonaparte, his name was, Fox recalled — and the French were being highly successful. But all these things, including the possibility of sudden and immediate action, faded in importance beside Fox's savage determination that his gun deck should be in absolutely perfect condition; the spilt mess meant far more to him, at that moment, than all the gallantry and glory that might lie over the horizon to leeward.

Being a gunnery officer was for Fox a pleasant occupation. He would have welcomed it even more had he had the opportunity to serve in the open air, handling the twelve pounders. He gave a quick but comprehensive scrutiny to the marine sentry standing guard on the companionway ladder, leading above decks. He looked a little green about the gills. Fox had no sympathy to waste on him. Provided he did his duty and prevented any seaman not authorized by Lieutenant Fox to leave his gun and go above decks, he could be made of green cheese for all Fox would care.

Everything seemed to be in order. Fox was too old a hand to be caught by mere semblances; but in the short time since he had managed to convince the despicably thick-headed authorities that he was a King's Officer (See "Fox 2: The Press Gang" also published by Thunderchild.) and had given his time and attention to training these men in the way he wanted a gun battery trained, he had improved the men at a thousand per cent. Oh, surely, they resented him, despised him, they had known him as one of themselves until that wild night they'd cut out *Narcissus*. But now he was moulding them. Fox tolerated nothing less than perfection when it came to guns and gunnery.

Right aft he turned about. He leaned past a gun and looked through the port, holding on to the tackle, but at this low a vantage point above the sea, which rolled away in a great washing of suds to leeward, he would be able to make out nothing of the chase. Still, he looked.

8

The men standing at the gun looked at him as he came inboard again; but he wasn't going to gratify their curiosity. And if one of them craned his fool neck out to find out what his betters on the quarterdeck were doing with the ship, Fox would have the hide off his back at the gratings tomorrow.

He had taken perhaps three steps forward when he heard a voice rumble something behind him. He turned around with a deliberate slowness. He looked back at the guncrew, rigid, immobile, their mouths compressed. Harideman, the gunner's mate in command of the four aft guns, was close by. Fox let his gaze fall on this unfortunate.

"Keep your crews quiet or every man jack of you will feel the cat tomorrow."

The men's faces did not change expression. They did not even blink.

This far aft the motion of *Tiger* was clearly apparent. The whole deck heaved up into the air as each long Atlantic roller passed away beneath her, moving from her starboard quarter diagonally across to her larboard bow. Fox didn't notice the movement except when any change in its regularity told him the ship was being worn or tacked or some weather change was upon them. With almost continual westerlies and with *Tiger* heading south and on the starboard tack, Fox could feel all he would ever allow himself to feel of jubilation at the thought that his larboard battery was on the lee side of the ship, and therefore the battery most likely to be brought into action during the chase. He could tell by that self-same motion of the ship that Captain Pulteney had set more canvas. The ship's motion increased in a pitching axis; but her rolling dampened off as she lay over to the breeze.

That motion upset the party climbing with panicky caution down the aft ladder. The rungs were narrow and set close together, although the ladder itself was wide enough to pass two men in opposite directions; it was no fancy

companionway with guard ropes and handropes. Fox heard a
shrill scream and then another, contralto, shriek.

He was at the ladder's foot in time to catch the mass of
descending petticoats, frocks, bonnets, gloves, stockings,
ribbons and laces that resolved itself, when he had unscrambled
it all, into two women. A maid's face in a mobcap showed
peering down with round eyes from the middle gun deck where
the twenty-fours were showing their teeth to the grey sea and
sky.

"Lawks a-mussy!" shrieked the maid. "They've broken
every bone in their poor bodies!"

Fox had a woman in each arm, his arms around their
waists as they sagged against him. Feathers tickled his nose and
perfume tried to cut a way through the bilge stink he seldom
noticed.

"Get down here, you baggage!" he roared. "Take these
ladies under your lee! Lively now!"

"Yessuh, surely suh," said the girl, and a white cotton
stocking showed as she put down her leg groping for the first
rung. Encumbered as he was, Fox could not help. The maid
was unused to the lower gun deck, that was obvious. The two
women — vastly different as he could tell — must be the
admiral's wife and the captain's — wife — and what the hell
those two antiques had any business in bringing women aboard
a man of war God alone knew.

"Give her a hand, Harideman!" Fox shouted. The
gunner's mate leaped to obey with an alacrity never shown
aboard ship except where grog or a woman or a started rump
were involved.

Fox was aware of the ludicrousness of the situation. He
was in command of a battery of fifteen thirty-two pounders and
might be required to open fire at any moment; and here he was
supporting two fainting women with his arms around their
waists as though they were strolling in Vauxhall Gardens.

The difference between the two women was startling. One, the vast and impregnable pile of rigid virtue, with a wide expanse of waist held firm by some female contraption, must be the admiral's wife. The other's waist was free from constricting apparatus, soft and yet firm, curved, yielding bouncily to the pressure of Fox's arm. She felt very good, did that one. She was the captain's mistress. Fox had not had the pleasure of meeting either of the ladies before. Tradition and influence and authority gave admirals and captains the sanction to take their women to sea, although the practice was dying out. And George Abercrombie Fox had not been honoured with an invitation to take dinner with either the admiral or the captain since his re-establishment to the quarterdeck.

The maid, with Harideman's solicitous assistance, had reached the deck. She clucked like a pregnant hen and rushed for Lady Creighton.

"There, there, y'r leddiship! We'll soon have you safe and sound below —"

The captain's coxswain and his servant now appeared on the ladder bearing sundry boxes and bales. Fox guessed with cynical contempt that the ladies had insisted on bringing all their little treasures with them as they dived down to the security of the aft orlop. He sniggered to himself. This meant real action, and in real action at sea there was no safe place aboard a wooden ship.

Lady Creighton was hauled free of Fox. Her grey india-rubber-like face with its multiple chins and toppling mass of artificial hair regarded him with glacial dislike.

Without a word she tottered off with the admiral's secretary, that vulture-necked individual, newly arrived below, supporting her to larboard and the maid holding on for mutual support to starboard.

Fox was left with the captain's light o' love. He looked at her — surprised that he could look down on her — and saw

11

her pale level eyes regarding him with a hint of mirth. Her lips were very red, soft and curved like a rosebud in the current fashionable mode. Her fair curls escaped in an abandoned confusion from her cap. He was suddenly aware that he was still clasping her waist, and that she was leaning against him, her soft breast thrusting in its muslin embrace against the coarse blue cloth of his uniform coat. Those bold brass crown and anchor buttons would be digging into white flesh — he shut his eyes, opened them, and she still hung on. Fox realised then that she knew exactly what she was doing and liking it.

He took his hand away and said formally: "Your pardon, ma'am. I trust you will be able to negotiate the rest of the way yourself."

"Thank you, lieutenant." Her voice was soft and breathy, with a tang of Cockney disguised by a honeyed hoarseness. "You are most kind." Her eyes devoured him. "It is Mr. Fox, is it not?"

He was startled — him, a crusty old shellback who was never surprised by anyone or anything in this man's Navy.

"At your service, ma'am."

"Ah!" she said, and the pink tip of her tongue flicked across those red lips. Her teeth, he noticed, were not attractive, only a little stained it was true; but snaggley and uneven. That brought that general Buonaparte to mind again, oddly; that whore he'd taken up with, Josephine, was said to have ugly teeth, or so the papers said.

A shout sounded from aloft and then the running patter of bare feet heralded the approach of a ship's messenger.

Fox smiled. He put a lot of himself into that smile. He made a little half-bow, oddly formal and yet, in its implications, outrageously immodest.

"I hope I may have the pleasure of making your acquaintance later, ma'am —"

She returned that smile. "Kitty Higgins, Mr Fox." And then, mysteriously, as she turned to go with a devilish gleam from the battle lanterns reflecting from her eyes, she added: "I recognise a compatriot when I meet one, Mr Fox."

She was gone, stepping daintily along the deck in satin slippers that old fool Captain Sir John Pulteney had paid two guineas a pair for in Bond Street. Fox dragged his mind away from her, from all the unfair distinctions in this life she stood for, and turned back to handling fifteen thirty-two pounder guns in battle.

Chapter Two

"Cock your locks! Fire! Stop your vents!"

The noise smashed in impossible volumes through the lowbeamed space. Acrid yellow gun-smoke gushed in colliding clouds as the big thirty-two pounders recoiled on their trucks and the smoke blatted against the sills of the gunports and billowed inboard. The blue battle-lanterns shed an eerie light on the scene. "Dante, thou shoulds't have been here," Fox said, out aloud, confident that in the bedlam no one would hear him revealing a weakness.

The main-deck twelve pounders had fired twice, earlier on, in an attempt to halt the chase. She hadn't hauled up and so the order had come for the middle deck's twenty-four pounders to join in, and now Fox's larboard big guns were in action. Fox felt fully alive, stretched, his intolerant eyes searching everywhere for the slightest fault in handling the guns, the slightest laxity. Mr. Midshipman Doyle and the two mates knew his ways, by now, and they jumped. The gun crews knew what would happen if they did not put every ounce into fighting the guns, and so they jumped, too.

Again the guns crashed out and roared back on their trucks, the bitter smoke gushing. Fox looked ostentatiously down at his watch, He kept a graven, sardonic look on his face. He knew these men. Just to spite him they'd work like demons to better their time.

The guns were wormed, sponged out with what the men called "woolly 'eaded bastards," loaded with cartridge, the shot wadded down, the action primed and then the gun captains grasped the lock-springs, awaiting Fox's order to fire. They'd be progressing to independent fire soon; Affleck, a gun captain with a sense of his own superiority, was usually the first. He'd rowed stroke oar when they'd cut out *Narcissus* and had been one of the most helpful of the hands during that hellfire time. But Gregory, now, was a gun captain who always seemed to experience difficulty in getting the best from his crew. Fox found time between the broadsides to wonder if Gregory would have to be replaced. No one and nothing would stand between Fox and absolute perfection.

Along the decks ran the powder monkeys, leaping from their ladders leading down to the magazines, dodging ringbolts and tackle, avoiding the capstan and the massive cables running lengthwise down the centre of the deck. Over on the starboard side Lieutenant Gloag and his gun crews could only stand in frustrated idleness. *Tiger* had begun with a hundred and fifty men above complement and although many of these had been lost in the usual round of sickness and accidents, and others had been sent away in prizes, she was still manned enough so that the big thirty-two pounders, at any rate, could be manned fully.

Fox had caught a quick glimpse of the chase through the forward gunport just before they'd come into action. She was a big French eighty-gun ship, and, as everyone knew, French eighties were every bit as powerful as British ninety-eights; more powerful, some said. With that turn of speed of which *Tiger* was capable the British three decker had outstripped the

16

seventy-fours in her squadron, and now she and the Frenchman were alone on the sea with the evening stealing in and the wind still fair from the west and the sea moderate and everything set for a night action.

Fox pursed his lips; and immediately smoothed them out again into a ruler-straight implacable line. Down here he must do his duty. There would be no opportunity for him to distinguish himself, unless he and some of his crews were called away for boarders. The hatred in him reared afresh at the thought. After he'd practically single-handed taken *Narcissus* back from the French, not only had he been in his view contemptuously refused a thirty guinea sword of honour from the Patriotic Fund, the Admiral had not even mentioned him in the letter he'd sent to My Lords Commissioners of the Admiralty. Fox would not see his name in connection with a glowing report in the *Gazette*. Unless your name went in the *Gazette* you were unknown, as good as dead and buried in a junior capacity in the Navy ...

He recalled with special vividness the affair of the 8th June of last year, when *Unicorn* took *Tribune*. It had been a hot fight and although *Unicorn* had not lost a man, *Tribune* had had thirty seven killed and Commodore Moulston and fourteen of the crew wounded. There had been praises all around, and promotions for the officers of the British frigate *Santa Margarita* which in an extension of the same action had taken the French *Tamise* — that had lately been the British *Thames*. Because the first lieutenant plus a number of prime seamen had been out of *Unicorn* sailing a prize, the second lieutenant had, clearly, taken over. But for the second lieutenant, William Taylor, there were kind words; but no promotion whatsoever. His captain had a knighthood. Down there in the lower gundeck George Abercrombie Fox found some good solid reasons for his cynicism about the bigwigs of the Royal Navy.

Further proof of that came as, echoing on the discharge of the next broadside from *Tiger,* an answering broadside from the Frenchman came smashing into the British three decker. Whoever was conning the ship had simply brought her up yardarm to yardarm and now stood back and left it to British gunnery to win the conflict. That British gunnery, given anything like an even chance, would always win had nothing to do with Fox's contempt for these so-called tactics. The French, as always, fired high to damage rigging and masts and thus cripple their pursuer so they could escape. But as the battle roared on and the ship lurched and juddered to the broadsides, more than one French ball thudded against *Tiger* along her row of lower gundeck ports.

Independent firing was ordered so the fastest guncrews could be let rip. Fox left Affleck and the other captains like him to get on with their job, and concentrated on urging on Gregory and the other slower teams. Gregory had a misfire; his flint failed to strike, or the spark failed to ignite the priming. Gregory stood, grimed, sweating, chest-heaving, for the moment at a loss in that infernal din.

"The match, you idiot!" Fox dashed up, yelling, grabbed a ready-lighted match from its notched water-tub. "What the hell are you waiting for, you misbegotten hunk of sheep's offal!"

The match ignited the priming and the big gun roared and reared back on its carriage. The barrels were hot now and the guns were leaping on their trucks like monstrous iron tigers.

A splintering crash — that typical, frightening sound of wood being split and sliced and scattered in every direction — burst in by the sill of the aftermost gun just as the gun captain jerked his lanyard.

Men shrieked as the splinters tore into them. The ring bolts had been smashed from the ship's side; massive timbers were wrenched loose and slivered into dozens of deadly weapons; the thirty-two pounder recoiled as it fired and the whole fifty-two hundredweight mass, powered by ten pounds of powder developing four hundred foot-tons of energy, surged back. The remaining shreds of tackle could not cope with that enormous force and they snapped with sounds lost in the uproar. The gun rampaged backwards rearing, leaping, its wheels scarcely touching the deck.

A man shrieked — once — as the monster cavorted over his chest. His squashed body looked like an obscene spider crushed beneath a careless foot. The gun collided with a stanchion, pulverised it, toppled, twisted, thundered directly for a powder boy with his leather bucket of cartridges just running up the aft ladder.

"Look out!" Fox roared. The boy saw even though he could not have heard Fox's yell in the bedlam. Like the monkey for which he was named the boy leaped sideways and sprawled across the cables down the centre of the deck.

The gun poised, emitting a rumbling from its trucks and a bell-like gong note from its barrel. Fox rushed across. Men were yelling, smoke billowed and stung his eyes — his eyes! Now, in this moment of supreme trial, his cursed left eye suddenly stung with a sharper pain than the acrid smoke could bring and he saw that damnable ring of purple and black begin to close around his vision.

He blinked — he knew that was useless, curse it! — and visualised with awful clarity what would happen if that monstrous gun fell down the hatchway. The ladder would be smashed to kindling in an instant. The gun would simply tear through the orlop deck like so much tissue and go on with its weight and momentum scarcely checked to punch a jagged hole in the ship's bottom.

After that the pumps could never cope with the inrush of water and *Tiger* would slowly settle in the sea until at last the waves crested in over the waist and quarterdeck and she would settle in a gurgle and rush in her last dive to the bottom.

They might be able to fother a sail over that jagged rent in her hull — they might manage to keep the water balanced with the pumps; but it was a task that would demand not only superhuman effort — that was required as a matter of course in the Navy — but also an immeasurable amount of luck.

Fox had never felt a particularly lucky individual.

His right eye peered desperately through the drifting veils of smoke. Up forward the steady successive beat of the guns firing reached him like a gale lashing a rock-bound coast. Men were running and yelling all about him.

The gun poised on the coaming.

"Unraffle that tackle!" Fox screamed, pointing to the next gun. Its captain saw at once and began reeving his tackle out. Fox tailed on to an end himself and ran, staggering, across to the hatch. As the ship moved in the sea the gun lurched against the coaming, tilting, and then falling back with a rumble of its trucks and a groaning from the deck timbers.

As a boy Fox had seen a twelve-pounder tear loose from its lashings during a gale and hurtle about the deck like one of those Spanish bulls the Dons used for the diabolical sport. Memory of that, of young Will and his legs crushed, drove him on. If only his right eye did not let him down now! He could see the tackle and the ringbolt and the harsh iron of the gun and he concentrated on what he must do — exactly, he supposed, as a matador must concentrate on the bull at the time of the kill.

His thoughts had raced ahead; barely half a second had elapsed since the gun tore free and at any moment it would tip and topple over. The ship heaved as the pattern of firing coincided and almost a full broadside tore in thunder and smoke from the iron lips of the guns.

Fox saw the gun teeter and slew, falling over sideways and jamming its carriage across the hatch coaming. The muzzle struck downwards, splintering the top couple of treads of the ladder. He hauled the tackle after him, leaning as though struggling against a wind. The barrel of the gun was now pointing at an angle down towards the bottom of the ship. If the trunnions broke free of the cap-squares and the gun took off, it would shoot down like a gigantic arrow.

Because of the heel of the ship to leeward the gun lay wedged on their larboard side of the hatch; Fox saw they would have to lift the thing to get it back on an even keel. This was not so much of a problem as the fear that the barrel would break free, for the Navy were nonchalantly used to handling enormous weights with blocks and tackle. He knew what he must do, the difficulty would be the doing of it.

Lieutenant Gloag from the starboard battery limped up; the wound he had sustained during the boarding of *Narcissus* had healed up nicely but had left him with a trifle of a limp. He was yelling and shouting at his men in his usual fashion. Fox ignored him. Anyway, he was senior to Gloag, so what the hell — at the moment the hole that might be punched in the ship's bottom concerned him most.

The ship heaved again and the wood of the trucks squealed against the wood of the coaming. Smoke drifted across. The blue lantern light made everybody's face a ghastly lead colour, as though newly-risen from their graves. Although — Fox heaved around the hatch dragging the clumsy tackle — although risen wasn't exactly the word in respect of graves applicable in the present circumstances.

He darted in at the gun and the ship skittishly chose that moment to plunge and he had to slide to a halt as the cascable moved with a sinister menace. The quoin had been knocked free and the trunnions were holding the gun barrel but there was no elevation-support from them; the gun, on its side, was swinging its barrel back and forward heavily, like the tongue of a monstrous lizard.

21

"Bring up more tackle, Mr Gloag," Fox yelled and then, added; "If you please."

The starboard side gunners were clustering now; more and heavier tackle was brought aft. Fox felt the surge of the ship beneath his feet and the whole tremor and tremble of *Tiger* transmitted through the soles of his feet interlocked in his brain with the broadside-interrupted rhythm of her motion. He looked down through the hatch past the iron barrel of the gun and saw the faces of those three stupid women staring up at him, their eyes and mouths like black holes cut out of sheets.

"Get away below!" he yelled. The idiocy of the remark fetched him. If the gun fell and crushed them they'd just die that much quicker, that was all. The maid was screaming — her throat was working convulsively and tears streamed from her eyes although he could not hear a sound from her — and Lady Creighton stood like a grey india-rubber doll, while Kitty Higgins was staring up in fascination, the tip of her pink tongue caressing those lips that looked bruised purple in the light.

They didn't move.

"Stand clear from under!" he bawled down.

Then there was no time for further thought of the women. The motions of the ship came together and instinctively, without having to calculate it out, that seaman's brain of his told him this was the time and he flung himself at the gun.

Now!

He hooked the tackle on, took up the slack and hauled back and twenty men seized on and tailed on behind him.

To hell with the carriage — that grim gaunt iron cannon was the danger. And then, in that moment, a French round shot tore in through the smashed port and mashed half a dozen of the men at the tackle. The rest writhed like a snake with its head crushed. The gun shifted; one trunnion hasp parted with a sharp crack clearly audible; the gun moved, slewing.

22

"Haul!" yelled Fox, feeling his arms tearing loose in their sockets. Men rushed across the blood and brains and intestines of their fellows smeared across the sand-strewn deck, tailed on. They took the strain. As the second trunnion hasp snapped and the gun hung free the men's biceps bulged, the tackle groaned, the ropes thrummed — then they had her.

"Heave!" Fox yelled. "Heave, you pile of cod-gutted bastards! *Heave!*"

Tailing on, throwing all the weight of their bodies on the cables, the men slowly walked back.

"Spikes!" Fox directed a party to spike and lever the gun over the coaming. Barrel and carriage were wedged between the forces of gravity seeking to drag the barrel down and the forces exerted by the men's muscles on the tackle. He shouted another party to snare the carriage; a rope around a truck hauled that up. With grunts and heaves and filthy abuse from Fox they got the gun back on to the deck. They chocked it up on a trunnion and then Fox saw the men lapsing, wiping the sweat and grime from their faces, beginning to realise the emergency was past.

But that emergency wasn't over for Fox, not by a long chalk. He was in command of fifteen guns, and by God! he'd have fifteen guns in action or know the reason why!

He routed out Harideman and told him to remount the barrel using tackle slung from an overhead beam. New cap-squares must be bolted on — a jury-rigged contraption it all might be — and damned dangerous, too — but that was what war was all about, in George Abercrombie Fox's book.

He lashed the men on and took time to go roaring forward to make sure Doyle and the mate up forward were doing their duty. The guns leaped and roared, the powder smoke billowed, the dead and wounded were dragged away and the powder boys leaped like monkeys through it all.

When he got back aft the barrel was being hoisted. Inch by half-inch it rose to be positioned over the righted carriage and slowly lowered. New hasps were fitted. He was sweating and shaking and his left eye's vision had completely gone now; but he hardly noticed any of that. He looked down the hatch and saw Kitty Higgins staring up, one hand on the ladder.

She said something; he could not hear what. Then — then she smiled and blew him a kiss.

Fox jerked back. Didn't she know there was a battle on? There was no time for that, not here on the lower gun deck of a line of battleship in action. He crossed to a port and looked out. The sun had almost gone, judging by the shadows and the French eighty-gun ship's side blazed golden in the last of the glow. No smoke puffs belched from her and Fox realised she hadn't been firing for some time.

It was with a sense of anticlimax that the order came down to cease fire. The Frenchman had struck. This action was all over. Honour, distinction, glory — none had been won this day by Fox — all he had done was his duty, which anyone else could have done, and which everyone was expected to do, come what might.

Chapter Three

In consequence of the successful action of *Tiger* in taking the French eighty-gun ship *Villeurbanne*, certain changes took place aboard. The admiral and the captain each received a sword valued at a hundred pounds from the Patriotic Fund; Sir Blundesely Creighton's certain peerage approached measurably nearer; Mr. Paunceford, the first lieutenant, had been promoted out of the ship — a compliment to his captain — and the officers and crew received the thanks of Parliament.

Fox spat on his palm. They knew what they could do with their thanks. Prize Money — that was what he was interested in.

Villeurbanne was so shattered that she would only be of use as a receiving ship, or a hulk, or a prison ship; but there was talk that the Admiralty would purchase her into the Service anyway and dole out a little Prize Money. After this year of the great mutinies times were changing in the Royal Navy. The capful of wind at the Nore had frightened those high and mighty lords and aristocrats. Oh, surely, they had hanged Richard Parker and put down the mutinies and they remained in their high offices with all their prerogatives and perks; but still and all, the common sailorman of England had spoken out. His fate now, like that of officers after the execution of Admiral Byng, was different. The lessons of Captain Bligh's famous mutiny had not been learned; now, at last, some glimmer of sense was being knocked into the bewigged heads of the lords of the land and sea.

Nelson had had his arm knocked off in that bungled affair at Santa Cruz, Teneriffe, and was invalided home. For Fox a macabre note was struck when he learned that the ship sunk by a large shot, sinking her instantly and destroying ninety-seven men, was named *Fox*. When introduced he was often accosted by a raised eyebrow and a scarcely veiled insolent attitude of inquisition accompanying the question: "Any relation of Charles James Fox." Fox would always answer carelessly, that he was not a relation. He had, because of the coincidence of name, followed Fox's career with an interest that did not extend to others. The politician's praise for the storming of the Bastille, his attitude of liberality towards the American colonies and his unusually generous view of life, made him for George Abercrombie Fox a man to whom he would not, all things considered, have minded being related. It would have brought him no advance or preference in the Service; he knew well enough what the fire-eaters thought of Fox; but it would in a very real sense have brought him satisfaction.... Then he would laugh at himself for an old fool, as though anyone in their right mind would wish to be associated with politicians!

Fox — the Charles James of the illustrious name — had married his mistress, Mrs. Armistead, in 1795 and was now living in near-retirement at Saint Ann's Hill hard by Chertsey and, so the papers said, had this year ceased to attend the House of Commons with any regularity. Thought of mistresses brought to Fox — the George Abercrombie out of that ilk — the remembrance of Kitty Higgins. Now there was a lass!

26

The feel of her firm and bouncy waist beneath his arm tingled and titillated him. That lush wench, Clara, whom he had rejected, had done nothing for him. Mind you, she had been some noblewoman incognito. That was enough to turn any man's manhood off.

The wardroom was now under the domination of Mr. Lockyer — the new first lieutenant. He was another of these sea-faring Lords so abominated by Fox; but he did have the courtesy to follow accepted Naval custom and drop the full use of his name — Lord Lockyer — for the more efficient and regular "Mister."

He was a disgustingly handsome individual with a virile face, curly dark hair, deep brown eyes and the manners of an angel. He was also personally extraordinarily brave. But he couldn't, as Fox well knew, navigate a toy-boat in a bathtub, and to handle the ship's sails he would tell the Master to get on with it and ostentatiously stalk about the quarterdeck with his telescope tucked under his arm like Anne Boleyn's head.

So that the wardroom became for Fox almost as much a purgatory as had been the lower deck; and certainly as much of a prison. He had to pay his whack for the extras brought out by the supply vessels, and the so-called president of the mess insisted that Fox cough up towards wine and other delicacies these high-flown individuals considered essential to sea duty.

During this period which saw *Tiger* refitted Fox took considerable delight in playing cards. He was always reluctant to play, making a good show of that, but always he took good care to play scrupulously fairly with his brother officers in like circumstances to himself. It was a strange thing, so the conversation went, how Lord Lockyer, and the honourable William Stanton, and Sir William Conyers, always seemed to lose when Fox played. Sir William Conyers was the marine captain and so, for a sailor, fair game. Fox would never cheat his comrades; for the aristocracy of ignorance he had no compunctions whatsoever.

The report he had put in about the runaway thirty-two pounder had been received and then, presumably, filed and forgotten. Still he had received no invitation to dine with either admiral or captain.

He thought that was carrying a grudge against him too far. It was good for naval discipline for the commanding officers to dine their officers by turn. Nelson did. All good commanders did. The scraggy lot aboard *Tiger* studiously left George Abercrombie Fox out of their little charmed circle.

Then someone took a hand to break through that charmed circle, and Fox, because he was irritated by the stupidities of those in authority, and because he wanted to get back at them, and because she was gorgeous, and because he felt like it, and anyway, just because, Fox, then, went along wholeheartedly with that breaking of barriers.

During the middle watch with the darkness of a cloud-covered sky falling to obscure even the quarterdeck rail from a half-dozen paces away, she crept out and caught his arm.

Fox jumped and looked down on her. She held one pink finger to her lips; the quartermaster at the wheel, the midshipman of the watch, the master's mate, the marine sentry — all the other people who had business on the quarterdeck of a line of battleship of His Britannic Majesty in time of war, all were within easy earshot. She pulled him back to the shadows, whispering fiercely.

"Why haven't you tried to see me, you big lummox?"

He felt bewildered. "How could I?"

"Not so loud, you big ox! How could you?" She half-turned so that her breast pushed into his uniform coat. That was no accident, even less so than the last time. "If you'd wanted to you'd have found a way."

He was jumping with anxiety now; his left eye began almost immediately to close around him that purple and black ring with its edging of pink. He grabbed her waist and pulled her to him. She wore a big boatcloak of some dark thick material; beneath it she wore a thin muslin dress so much like the one worn by Clara back at Plymouth on that night in the inn. He swallowed and bent his head.

"Of course I wanted to see you — all of you! But I'm a junior lieutenant — you're the captain's lady —"

She nudged him. "Thank you for your kind opinion of me, sir."

"Kitty, Kitty — if you're caught —"

"If I'm caught, so what? The old fool would kiss my arse and think he was in heaven no matter what I told him. Aren't you my cousin, then?"

Fox chuckled, low. There was a way, then. He squeezed her waist and felt that thrill shoot up his spine.

"So — fine; so how do you suddenly announce this?"

"Leave it to me — Foxey." She reached up slid an arm around his neck and drew him down. Her lips were soft and warm and trembling and sweet — sweet!

She broke away and, for a moment, she shuddered.

"What — ?"

"No, Foxey, my gallant blade. I'm from the Old Kent Road — my sister goes whoring down there still. I was lucky. I found a protector and worked my way up to being Sir bloody John bloody Pulteney's little *poule.*" She drew her breath again.

"They're a bunch of rat-bags aboard here, ain't they just! That new first lieutenant — ain't he a darling, tho? — they put in in place of old Poncey." That would be Lieutenant Paunceford, Fox realised, and smiled in the darkness. "He's had a try at me virtue —"

"Oh?"

She sniggered. "I put my ladylike knee where it'd do the most good. Ain't 'ad no trouble from 'im no more!"

"Kitty, my little Kitty — your Old Kent Road is slipping out and your Government House is losing —"

"Cor, strike a light! Don't I 'ave enuff trouble wi' all that poncy way o' talk wivaht you remindin' me?"

He chuckled and instantly stilled and looked about. Only the usual shipboard noises sounded; but he had been away too long. The marine sentry was only a few paces off. Fox bent his head again and sucked greedily on those ripe soft lips, his hands squeezing her breasts, so firm and full and altogether delightful. She pulled away, breathless.

"Foxey, old sport —"

"I must go —"

"I was right," she said, drawing the boat cloak around her. "You're the dirtiest old man among 'em all — and the one I'd pick if we were cast adrift in an open boat!"

She was gone.

Fox, still dizzied by the sweetness and scent of her, compressed his lips, straightened his spine, stalked back across the quarterdeck and rasped out with calculatingly insulting a tone his necessary but superfluous orders — aboard a King's Ship events progress according to the half-hour sandglass or the officer of the deck will want to know why.

Just how she worked it Fox never knew; but two days later he received an invitation to dine with the captain. Dinner, as was the custom, took place about half-past three in the afternoon. The wind was from the west, a more or less usual quarter, but the sea was a little choppy and *Tiger* beat up on the larboard tack on her eternal watch and ward. Fox had had sent out to him a new uniform among the packets on the supply vessels, paid for from money promised from pay and prize, and he dressed with a fastidiousness that made his marine servant fidgety.

"God blast your eyes, man!" snapped Fox, ripping his stock open. "Tie all that furbelow rubbish again, and this time do a seamanlike job on it, curse you for a masquerading lobster!"

He felt no anger towards the marine; the man was just doing the job to which he had been assigned; the days when non-combatant servants were carried aboard being dead and gone and servants now being expected to be of use during action at sea. The marine stolidly retied the stock and cravat and Fox harrumphed and, precisely on time, went through to the captain's aft cabin.

Sir John Pulteney greeted him with an effusive warmth Fox put down to Kitty's influence. Certainly taking *Narcissus* — that had once been the French *Mortagne* — and salvaging that bottom-breaking thirty-two pounder had never brought out this amount of friendliness in the captain before.

The first lieutenant, Mr. Lockyer, and the marine captain, Sir William Conyers, had also been invited. As well there was a young snotty — Mr. Midshipman Doyle. Fox kept his face straight when he saw him. He had his own opinion of that young gentleman, and he felt that Kitty would be well advised to beware a groping hand up her petticoat if Doyle was around.

The dinner of delicacies bought especially for the captain's table passed off pleasantly enough. If Fox ate like this all the time he'd develop a decided paunch very quickly. There were fresh mutton, eggs, some green vegetables, and a wine that had made a circuitous route from Republican France across the channel by *chasse marée* and up to some Squire's cellars and then back again to Plymouth and so out to the British Fleet blockading Republican France. Fox sighed and drank the wine — which was poor stuff compared with rum — and decided to forget cares of high strategy that did not make sense and concentrate instead on this new cousin of his.

She looked charming, gay and light-hearted, in her white muslin dress that did, at least, have the decency to be not quite transparent enough to show her nipples. She laughed a lot and Fox, uneasily, guessed she had something planned and was highly-strung as a consequence.

Pulteney started off by announcing that the supply vessel had brought news of a great engagement with the Dutch about four leagues off the Wykerdens. Admiral Duncan, that conspicuously large admiral, had met and signally defeated a Dutch fleet under Vice Admiral de Winter. It had been a confused battle; but of one fact there could be no doubt; the British had won.

"This frees our northern problems," said Pulteney, with satisfaction. "Now we can turn our attention to the French in the Mediterranean. Since they turned us out we must go back. Admiral Jervis — Lord Saint Vincent, I suppose I must say — will not be denied that now."

The others nodded. Pulteney went on, speaking with his mouth full: "A strange fact of the battle with the Dutch is that not one of our ships lost so much as a topmast. The Dutch suffered severely, in hulls and rigging; but they seem to have fired only at our hulls."

"Not like the French," commented Lockyer, primly swallowing before speaking. "We must give thanks that they always try to smash our spars whilst we are knocking merry hell out of them."

Fox remained silent. He had seen the bloodstained decks of French men-of-war after actions; they were the enemy, men he was paid to fight; but they fought bravely according to their lights. He'd not knock Monsieur Jean Crapaud or impute cowardice to him.

The thing he perhaps objected to most was their habit when surrendering of firing a broadside into an English ship and then immediately hauling down their colours, so as to avoid return fire. They called it honour of the flag, or something. He wondered what he'd do in those circumstances.

When the dinner party broke up, Kitty spoke quietly to Pulteney, who turned to Fox, saying with all his grey leaden gravity. "Mrs Higgins would like to have a few words with you, Mr Fox. Your mothers were sisters, it seems, and she has had no word from her for some long time. It is, it seems to me, Mr Fox, very remiss of you not to have written."

"Yes, sir," said Fox. He spoke meekly. "I do admit to error there, sir, and I am truly sorry for it."

"Ha, harrumph," said Pulteney, in his officious way.

Kitty had a small suite of rooms, just a sitting room, a bedroom, and a dressing room, all tiny boxes, off the starboard side of the captain's quarters, and here the bulkheads would be torn down when the ship cleared for action, as everywhere else in the ship. She closed the door and at once turned towards Fox, her hand to her lips, her eyes alight, her whole body animate with feverish passion.

He didn't notice the furnishing, he didn't notice anything except her — her dress was off, her petticoats were off, she was standing there, naked beneath the lamp, before he had time to catch his breath.

"My God, Kitty," he breathed. "You're beautiful!"

So began a different period in Fox's life that he knew could not last; that he seized with both hands, that he gloated over during every minute of every day.

When the chill Atlantic mist crept down around *Tiger* and he was standing the middle watch she would slip out to their favourite spot in the shadows of the break in the deck. She would wear a thick boatcloak and Fox would feel her nakedness beneath if as he lifted her petticoats and as the ship plunged beneath them they let themselves go to that living rhythm. They could not do this when there was the slightest chance of being seen. They would go to her tiny cabin to talk about their relations, and they would talk, but of themselves and of their lives and their hopes and aspirations. Kitty's view was essentially simple. She was beautiful. Incredibly beautiful. So she knew that in ten, fifteen years, she would not be beautiful. She had to make her fortune, enough to live on, before her beauty faded and she could find no more protectors. She made no bones about it. Fox warmed to her. He knew he did not love her, although that would have been an insanely easy thing to do. But he felt an obsessive affection for her, he was debauched by her, he could not have enough of her, and, too, he respected her for her straightforwardness, her honesty, the clear-sighted way in which she faced what life had presented her with and made of it something that, if she could not be proud, at least she need not be ashamed.

It could not last.

They were discovered in *flagrante delicto* by Pulteney opening the door. Fox climbed down as Kitty smoothed down her petticoats covering up her long white legs and Fox turned with a lopsided smile, waiting for the axe to fall.

Chapter Four

"Her cousin?" said Vice-Admiral Sir Blundesely Creighton. He was thoroughly enjoying himself. "In *flagrante?* Aboard *Tiger?*"

The leaden-hued countenance of Captain Sir John Pulteney had deadened to a more livid hue. He kept on opening and closing his hands as though Fox's neck was between his constricting hands.

"Dangling from the yard arm," he said, the words coming out like a cockerel's strangled last gasp. "Let him dance on air — that's what I'd like to do!"

"I've an idea that Naval Rules and Regulations may not quite — ah, quite — cover this kind of incident, my dear Sir John." The admiral spoke suavely. His own wife was so impregnable a rock he wondered why he bothered to bring her to sea with him; he had a vague idea it was at her suggestion and, seeing Kitty Higgins, he also had another vague idea that his wife's reasons had to do with *poules* like Kitty.

"Can't we have the marines shoot him?" asked Pulteney.

The admiral felt relief. The captain might be the bane of his life, they might detest the sight of each other; but at last Sir

John was showing a grasp of the true situation. If the Fleet heard of this — cuckolded, horned by his own mistress — Sir John's tenuous authority would be dissipated. There would be no spectacular exhibition of mutiny, for example; but that spiritual exercise of absolute authority would be damaged. It would have to be managed quietly.

"What about Mrs. Higgins, Sir John?"

"Oh, she has a contrite heart, the poor girl." Pulteney reflected on the tearful scene. "She was seduced away. There can be no doubt of that."

Creighton reflected that the gallant captain did not wish to be deprived of his comforts for the rest of his commission. An eminently sensible attitude.

"Very well, then," he said, brisking together the papers on his desk. "The young gentleman had better be transferred out of *Tiger*. You'll write him off your muster book, Sir John." He chuckled. "I fancy Tranter can make use of him."

Sir John Pulteney let his lined mouth relax into a smile. It was a parody of what a smile should be; but it accurately reflected Pulteney's feelings.

"Yes, sir. *Sheridan* is noted in the Fleet. I think Captain Tranter will be very good for Mr. Fox."

The Vice-Admiral had been highly amused by the whole incident. He did not envy anyone serving under Captain Tranter of *Sheridan;* but that young rip Fox deserved all he got. He also reflected that under another captain *Tiger* would be a much more happy ship. He sighed. They couldn't all be Nelson's or Collinwood's or Troubridge's.

Lieutenant Lord Lockyer conveyed the information to Fox.

"I don't know what you've done, Mr. Fox. I have never really understood just how it was you came to have the honour to serve aboard the flagship in the first place. But I cannot say I envy you your transfer to *Sheridan.*"

Fox breathed out, then in, held the breath, then breathed out again. So he'd been let off. Oh, surely, *Sheridan* was an ugly ship, a seventy four with a bad reputation; but at least his career had not been ruined. It had suffered a check, it had not been blighted.

His few items of baggage were whipped down into the jolly boat and he descended the side and settled in the sternsheets. Affleck was rowing stroke. Fox looked at that idiotically cheerful face with its tufty eyebrows and the man's biceps that bulged so powerfully and at his smart flagship-style clothing — blue jacket and white ducks — and he sighed. He'd never had a tie-mate aboard *Tiger* — a mate to whom he would turn automatically for the mutual tie-ing operations that gave their name to that special dual comradeship — but he remembered now that Affleck more than anyone else had seemed to be there to help him. Surely, Fox wasn't getting maudlin in his old age? A loner, was Fox, a man alone; always had been and always, it seemed, would be. Since the death of Captain Cuthbert Rowlands, who had made him what he was in a naval sense, he had found no one in whom he could place trust or even affection. Except for his family, and they were his whole burning reason for existing and submitting to the irrational tyranny of the Navy.

The jolly boat bounced over the chop and Fox was aware that telescopes would be trained on that dancing little craft and speculation would be sweeping the ships of the squadron. The Navy was an enclosed environment in which rumour and scandal grew luxuriantly like the jungles he'd seen in Central America, creating a life and world far-removed from the comprehension of land lubbers.

Sheridan loomed over him now, and he took the opportunity to study the seventy four. She was ugly, there was no gainsaying that. Her bluff bows indicated she was of Dutch origin, which would also, presumably, mean she was of shallow draught to negotiate the shoals around that country so recently drubbed by Admiral Duncan, and that would mean she'd be a cow against the wind with enough leeway on her to drown Cowley's tap-room. She'd been painted an ochreish yellow-brown all over and she looked lumpy, squat, completely without the redeeming features that made a ship-of-the-line so beautiful an object in the eyes of observers ashore who remained in wilful ignorance of the squalid and horrendous conditions aboard.

Her sails, slatting now she was hove-to awaiting his arrival, looked old and tattered, their colour that of a dungheap with looping curves of dampness blotching their heads, the tattered effect optical only. Fox knew that every shot-hole or weakness would be thoroughly patched by the sail-maker and his mates, or the first lieutenant would have their hides off their backs.

The jolly boat rounded to and without a single moment's hesitation Fox leaped and scrambled up the ship's side and dived through the entry port. For him, of course, there were no shrills on the boatswain's pipes, no clash as the marines presented arms, no sideboys in their white gloves to hand him up. He was just a lieutenant.

His baggage was whipped up and followed him on to the deck. He turned to see the coxswain take the tiller and give the order to give way. Affleck bent to his oar. Fox suddenly felt that he was leaving something behind.

Kitty — Kitty would be all right. If he had seemed not to concern himself over her it could only be because he had faith in her beauty and wit and powers of persuasion. She'd have that old fool Captain Sir John Pulteney eating out of her hand, with even greater dotage than before. Kitty — Kitty ... If he could ever be said to miss anything he knew he'd miss Kitty as he'd never missed any person outside the family and Captain

Rowlands before. Even Sally for whom he'd cherished a sickly devotion paled in comparison.

Fox reported himself to the first lieutenant, a Mr. Frobisher. With a name like that the man surprised and dismayed Fox. He greeted Fox civilly enough; but although he had a high colour, and full cheeks, and looked strong and capable still, he was considerably older than Fox and in his eyes there lurked a strange shifty expression that made Fox realise immediately that all the stories he had heard about *Sheridan* must be true.

Captain Tranter was notorious as one of the famous mad captains of the Navy List.

The stories of the mad captains were legion. Taking watch and watch about, so that a man was on duty twelve hours out of every twenty four, was a mild method they had of displaying their absolute authority. They could order their officers to be called every hour on the hour. They could devise all manner of grotesque functions for officers and men and there was no authority in the ship to say them nay. The breeze at the Nore had not yet blown away this kind of mad captain in the Royal Navy.

Fox made a deliberate decision. He made up his mind that he'd have to take whatever was coming — and then immediately determined he'd fix Tranter's wagon if the maniac bothered him overmuch. Fox had his ways.

When he made the acquaintance of Tranter the encounter left Fox absolutely determined not to put up with the man for an instant longer than he had to. The whole ship was in a state of fear. There was only one way they could deal with a captain on the high seas — and although mutiny was fashionable this year, the spirit of the men aboard *Sheridan* was such that the mere thought of mutiny left them pale and trembling.

Tranter was thin and gaunt, with a rim of grey stringy hair, eyes like pinchbeck, and a mouth like the cutwater of a shark. He dressed in foppish taste with a profusion of gold lace, he stank of a heavy scent, and his hair — what there was of it — was pomaded and perfumed. He habitually walked with his hands in their fancy ruffles clasped behind his back, his head thrust forward, and a rim of red showing beneath those strange eyes. He looked Fox up and down, said: "Ha harrumph!" which was the standard method of conversation of many officers, looked over at *Tiger* leading the line, brought his gaze back to Fox, and said: "I believe one of my pigeons has settled in the foretop, Mr. Fox. Do you kindly run and bring it to me."

Fox ran along the gangway, jumped into the fore ratlines and went up hand over hand, feeling the blood coursing through his body and, despite the insanity of the order, joying in the exercise. Of course, the foretop was as devoid of pigeons as were the maintop and mizzentop. He did not hurry about coming down. He stayed up there alone — the lookout was perched in the maintop which on British ships, even this re-rigged Dutch wallower, would be considerably higher than the foretop — until he figured that Tranter would either have forgotten what it was he'd sent Fox to do, or that he would be so primed with explosive anger he would be malleable. George Abercrombie Fox was well aware just how dangerously he was playing with fire. Any other man would have scampered up the shrouds, given a quick look around the foretop, and probably have slid down the backstay to save time in getting back to the quarterdeck. Fox counted on that.

He descended the ratlines, ran back up the gangway, conscious of the eyes of the men on deck fixed on him like leeches. He approached Tranter, saluted formally, and said: "Lieutenant Fox reporting, sir."

Tranter had not forgotten the errand.

"Well, Mr. Fox? Did you find my pigeon?" His misty regard searched Fox.

"You did not say, sir, if the pigeon you required me to find was brown or white."

Fox stood quite still, his face perfectly composed, politely waiting.

Tranter opened his mouth, all ready primed to blast at Fox in response to the excuse he had firmly expected. He slowly shut that mouth until its shark-like hardness tautened the muscles along his jaw. He clasped his hands into the small of his back and, his head thrust down, took a turn or two up and down his quarterdeck between the carronade slides and the ringbolts in the deck. He approached Fox again.

"If I said it was neither brown nor white, Mr. Fox?"

"There was no grey pigeon there, either, sir."

"Ha harrumph."

Again that stumping pouter-pigeon walk. Fox had to fight the giggles at that particular comparison. Here was Tranter back again, his red-rimmed eyes cunning.

"You obtained a post on the flagship, Mr Fox; yet they send you to me. I need first class officers in my ship, sir, not fancy popinjays appointed through influence and petticoat government who are unable to calculate, do not know a sheet from a brace, and are good only for boating — assuming that they live long enough for that. What are you, Mr. Fox?"

"I have no influence whatsoever, sir, and arrived in *Tiger* by chance." Fox let his calculating mind free rein, and decided not to chance agreeing with this captain. He did agree with him; but any extra word would lay him open to charges silence would prevent.

"I'd have all those fancy popinjays struck from the List." Tranter swung away and stalked towards his cabin. Fox could only hope that mad captain had forgotten him. Then a new and horrible thought occurred to Fox. This mad captain hated authority — it oozed from him. But Fox hated authority too, detested and despised the nincompoops and incompetents set over him by influence, yet he looked forward to gaining his step, to being posted captain, to walk his own quarterdeck. When he had achieved that would he, too, be as mad as this mad Captain Tranter? The prospect chilled him.

Mr. Frobisher looked shiftily at Fox.

"I don't know how you did that, Mr. Fox. But you're the first officer joining — well, never mind. You'd best go below and sling your hammock."

So began a fresh and brisking time for Fox as the dregs of the old year ran out, for he was constantly on the alert for the slightest fault, ever ready to anticipate problems, keeping as far to windward of the captain as he could — even though aboard a King's Ship the captain always strode the windward side of his quarterdeck — Fox was dealing in matters metaphysical.

The idea that he might end up like Tranter — if he was lucky — and like Frobisher if he was not, obsessed him more and more. The ship was a floating hell, its atmosphere far different from the squalid carelessness of *Tiger,* and he knew that he must get away very quickly before he was irredeemably corrupted.

There were many floggings.

Fox shared the general Navy view that discipline must be maintained at all costs; and flogging was the accepted way. Certainly, most of the men themselves agreed, albeit reluctantly, that it was better to be flogged, quick and over and done with, than to be sentenced to rot in a prison cell where they would waste away to a sickly and unpleasant death. Prison punishment could kill the British seaman. A flogging round the Fleet, on the other hand, aroused fierce contempt in Fox for the humanity and sanity of my Lords Commissioners of the Admiralty. After three or four hundred lashes a man was just about done for, seven or eight hundred if they did not kill then and there left the man useless to himself and to the Navy and to the country. Fox witnessed punishment a hundred times without wincing; a single flogging around the Fleet put him off colour for days, with a deep inward contempt for himself he could not rationalise out no matter how he tried.

Why should he think of flogging and Kitty Higgins in a grotesque juxtaposition? For the first time he really looked squarely at the incredible fact that Kitty had given herself to him at all. She didn't love him. Why him of them all aboard *Tiger?* Surely it could not just be as simple as her need for someone of her own class? One thing he did know; he ached for the feel of her now, aboard *Sheridan,* with a crazy captain doing his best to make life even more of a misery than life at sea always was.

During this period aboard *Sheridan* with its monotony of blockade duty and its sudden squalls and its endless beating to and fro and its always demanding vigilance there came to Fox a clammy sense of the way his life was pre-ordained into a set routine. He had to get out of this ship. As the new year wore on rumours continually swept the squadron and the Fleet of great moves and vast combinations of the enemy. This general Buonaparte, who had cleared Italy and who by his mere threat had tumbled the British out of the Mediterranean, bore all the marks of a mad dog on the rampage and it was as certain as anything in war ever could be that he'd be off attacking fresh victims and amassing more glorious victories in the very near future.

Supply packets brought news out to the ever-vigilant blockading squadrons. Mingled with the absorbing fragments of world-news were those other items of delicious gossip — how a Mrs. Bradleyman had murdered all her eleven children in Fames Lane and hidden the pitiable bodies in the attic and behind the wall-panelling and under the floorboards, and of how the faithful pet-dog of one of them, little Alice, had so sniffed and whined at the cellar-door as to alarm the neighbours and lead to the horrible discovery — of how a mail coach had run away outside Westgate and crushed to death a party of clergymen inspecting the ruins of the ancient abbey there — of how the various victims had comported themselves at Tyburn Tree. Fox could always cast a proprietary eye over those hanging reports, for hadn't he been named for his Uncle Abercrombie, who had achieved immortality himself by being hanged at Tyburn?

With the same urgency as Fox wished to get out of Captain Tranter's *Sheridan,* Admiral Creighton wanted to get Captain Tranter's *Sheridan* out of his squadron. Fox welcomed the possibility of some relief from tedium when orders came to wear away north and assist in one of the periodic landings made on the continent. They usually turned out disastrously; but Britain had no other way of flexing the muscles of her soldiers.

The plan called for the descent on Banquarie, the seizure of the mole and the destruction of the dock facilities there. A flat sandy beach extended eastwards from the harbour and lofty chalk heights dominated the whole area from the south and west. A motley collection of vessels had been assembled at Margate but *Sheridan,* coming up from the south, was in time only to escort them for the last few miles before the landing. Fox leaned on the rail and stared over the grey swell at the untidy procession of sail. The lobsters would be heaving their guts out aboard the transports. He felt no elation, now, only a chill premonition that once again England was dissipating her strength in penny packets against the frightening strength of the continent.

Chapter Five

As the soldiers were ferried ashore on to the flat and exposed sandy beach, Fox thought how much their red coats at this distance looked like flakes of blood.

The expedition consisted in the main of the light companies drawn from a variety of regiments, under the command of General Folsham, amounting to about a thousand men, with four guns. The Navy's contribution, apart from the handful of transports, a thirty-two gun frigate, *Epernave,* and the seventy-four *Sheridan,* consisted only of a couple of bomb-ketches, a cutter and a ten-gun brig.

The wind blew with a force that indicated it would increase before it decreased, driving low grey clouds up from the southwest. If it shifted southerly the expedition would be trapped in the shallow bay formed between the chalk heights of Saint Michel to the southwest and the promontory of the calanques up to which the beach curved. Already the long white strips of breaking waves surged up the beach, one after the other, like successive lines of charging white-maned cavalry. The boats took the men in and without undue mishap the expedition huddled on the shore, the troops, miners, the four guns and the artillery, some stores and three hundred barrels of gunpowder. Acting with some vigour General Folsham set off to make the first attack on the works covering the mole.

Together with the bomb ketches, *Sheridan* and *Epernave* moved in cautiously to cover the advance with their guns. The fortifications opened up as soon as the British ships were well within range and for some time a hot fire was exchanged. Fox had been appointed to command *Sheridan's* starboard main deck twelve pounders. He relished, at least, being in the open air, although he was aware that the massively thick hull of *Tiger's* lower gun deck did not stand between him and the enemy's fire.

Captain Tranter had put on full uniform. He strode his quarterdeck, sniffing the air, and every now and then declaring he smelled victory, called for a fresh cigar which was immediately brought on deck for him by Hannibal, his black servant.

Smoke began to cover the earthworks but the wind was able to sweep away most of the smoke higher up. Fox could sometimes make out the red dots that were the men of the British flank companies as they advanced. For some time the issue was in doubt.

The speed with which the landing had been made and the rapidity of the advance, together with the brisk fire maintained by the covering ships, brought success to the army, and by late afternoon Fox could see red dots on the earthworks and the stone battlements beyond and then, as though to make absolutely sure, the Union Flag rose jerkily up a flag-staff in the centre. Captain. Tranter emitted a puff of smoke and then, with obvious reluctance, ordered the cease fire. For the first time, to Fox, the mad captain had seemed almost human.

With the cessation of fire that otherworldly silence crept back to deafen eardrums accustomed to blocking out sheer waves of sound. Tranter turned to his first lieutenant with an order that Fox did not hear about his pigeons. Frobisher at once ran forward to the quarterback rail and bellowed for Mr. Blount. Mr. Midshipman Blount, a weasel-faced lad, although he could not, Fox had previously observed, help that facial impediment, was a morose individual who clearly should have taken up an office life in Mincing Lane.

"Mr. Blount!" yelled Mr. Frobisher. "Kindly take yourself up to the maintop and see that the capt'n's pigeons are all safe! Lively, now!"

"Aye, aye, sir!" shouted Blount, and without a word or a bye-your-leave to Fox, under whose orders he had just been commanding six of the twelve-pounders, he leaped for the main shrouds and went up as though musketry had been opened on his exposed rear-end. Fox kept all expression off his face. He'd seen two men flogged for disbelieving in the captain's pigeons.

Blount yelled down. "All safe and sound, sir! Not a feather disturbed!"

Captain Tranter took another puff on his cigar and then observed, with the air of a man hearing his wife and family have been rescued from a flood: "Heaven be praised, Mr. Frobisher. My little darlings have as great an aversion to gunfire as I have a fondness for it."

"Yes, sir," said Frobisher. Like Blount, he knew how to handle the pigeon business. "I fancy the wind is shifting and your pigeons will be happy to remain at home."

It was always "your" pigeons — never "the" pigeons.

Fox looked up at the vane atop the mainmast, just visible from where he stood, *Sheridan* having entered action with topsails, the driver and a couple of headsails only set. The vane was swinging, erratically, as though the wind that was to come was sending out outriders. But the vane was clearly swinging to southerly.

47

A vast explosion boomed at them from the shore. A spout of smoke and rock and debris flew up from the area hidden by the mole. The men gave a cheer. Any kind of bang, provided it didn't do them any harm, was good for a little spontaneous letting off of energy.

Whatever dock facilities Banquarie had once boasted, she possessed them no longer.

Further explosions followed and flames and smoke began to lift from that shore. The soldiers were going about their business of destruction with deliberate purpose. Fox glanced up at the wind vane again. When he looked back to the beach the surf had grown in intensity and violence, the white marching lines hurling themselves up the flat sand with a remorselessness no sailorman could ignore.

Surely the red-coated, red-necked soldiers would see? Commodore Sharp, aboard the frigate *Epernave,* was the senior naval officer, and he must see. Yes — there went the bundles up his signal halyards. When they burst Fox needed no signal book to guess the import of their orders. If the soldiers didn't embark now they never would.

The naval signal party ashore would have a little difficulty in reading the flags, for with the wind as it was the flags would be blowing almost directly at them; but signal midshipmen were notoriously ingenious and would find a way. Answering flags broke the signal mast erected ashore. Dark figures astride horses reared and then pounded off inland. A quickened activity was apparent among the men left by the stores on the beach and among the boats drawn up from the surf.

Fox was suddenly profoundly glad he was not among that landing party.

He began to think that the weather had shown every sign of worsening for the past twenty four hours; a southerly breeze hereabouts usually meant fine weather; but with the Equinox not far off freak effects had to be figured into the calculations. Whoever was in command — and whilst he thought of General Folsham and Commodore Sharp his mind flew instinctively to those grim and distant Lords of Admiralty in Whitehall — should have had the courage to have postponed the operation. Was blowing up a tiny dock worth the lives or captivity of a thousand English soldiers and the equivalent of a ship's company of seamen? In Fox's book he didn't think so. That, he knew, marked another of his weaknesses. He remembered how he'd dived into the water to rescue young Tommy and in so doing endangered the successful dropping of that spy in the mouth of the Laronne. Roland, that was the spy's name. Fox knew his own weaknesses. He often felt that if his superiors discovered them as well as he would never achieve post rank, let alone fly his own flag.

The ship's company of *Sheridan* still stood at quarters, and Tranter clearly had no intention of ordering the watch below to dismiss for supper. They'd stand by their guns all night if need be. That, to Fox, was understood, a way of life in the Navy, something he might do himself without a second thought. It had no relation to throwing away the lives of valuable men.

If the wind increased very much more and also shifted to a few points east of southerly then all the ships here would be on a lee shore and in immediate peril. Fox began to calculate out what he would do if he was in Commodore Sharp's fancy gold-buckled shoes.

The minutes ticked by. Darkness would fall soon and then, assuming Sharp had made no signals, Tranter would be at liberty to think of the safety of his ship first. He would have to beat out and make some searoom, that was the first thing any sailorman considered.

Now along the mole and trudging rapidly across the beach came the first of the troops. They moved with a steady jog-trot over the sand. Fox could see the red lines lengthening. They had wounded with them. Everything at the beach was in readiness for instant embarkation.

Away over to their left, below the heights of Saint Michel, the whole chalk face lit with a golden glow as the lowering sun fell upon the westward precipices, leaving the eastern face in shrouding darkness. But from that shadow, long vivid tongues of flame pierced out and the sullen rumble of big guns rolled towards them.

The shots fell wide of the troops mustering on the beach. But the French persisted in their artillery bombardment, and Fox began to chafe at his own ship's inaction. Surely, Sharp must do something, and do it soon?

Abruptly a file of men waiting to board a boat were swept away. Bits and pieces of equipment and bodies and muskets showered across the sand. Fox felt the anger in him, the frustration of knowing he, personally, could do nothing to prevent this waste. And now, surely and with increasing strength, the wind was backing, going from southerly to east-south-east, and the velocity rose up the scale with that shift in direction. Now all along the beach wind and tide struggled at right angles, the surf reared and roared and the few boats which had pushed off swung crazily. Fox saw one boat swing, tip, he held his breath, and then the boat heaved over and in a welter of sprawling blue and white bodies and red bodies, sailors and soldiers were pitched into that murderous surf.

Fox's hands gripped into fists on the rail.

The rest of the boats were not putting off. The wind shrieking through the rigging, the way *Sheridan* was bucking the sea, the foaming confused mass of whitecaps, all told eloquently that those men ashore would not be got off this night.

Now the commodore was signalling again, the flags barely readable in the fast-fading light. "Make all sail conformable to weather conditions." Well, that was clear enough.

The little flotilla would have to beat out and make an offing, then with enough sea room between them and the shore they could ride out the night. When they returned in the morning, what would they find? Paris was not so many leagues away on a postroad from Banquarie, and there were bound to be garrisons of Republican soldiers on that road within easy marching distance. The English had blown up some installations and no doubt destroyed a number of barges that might have been used in the possible invasion of England; but the price was too high, in George Abercrombie Fox's book, many lives too high.

The Navy ruled the seas, so the British said. Well, then, let the French come out. The Royal Navy would destroy them on the seas, as it had destroyed invasions on the seas before.

Now the darkness was made darker by rolling masses of cloud that hid the stars. The Master, to whom Captain Tranter entrusted all the navigation and sailing of the ship, took *Sheridan* out smartly enough, heeled over under the minimum of canvas.

The men were stood down. Fox could throw himself into his cot-hammock for an hour or two before being called out at midnight for the middle watch.

Once the ships of the flotilla had cleared the land they could lay to in the sea and spend a comfortable night. Their lights bobbed in regulation-spaced intervals. The night with its wind and waves passed for the ships as many another night had passed during this war. They were in no danger from the elements, the wind, having continued to back and blowing from the north-east, dropped much of the power and violence of the earlier hours, and, as for their human enemies, although the lookouts kept alert no one in his right mind expected the French to venture out. Everyone wanted them to, of course, the sublime confidence of the British seaman in his own seamanlike qualities giving him an unquestioning and unshakeable faith in himself.

That change in wind direction was the first thing Fox noticed as he came on deck in the dawn. He checked out the exact times and the wind values, and then he looked across at the beach, and pulled in his lower lip over his teeth. The flotilla had not done a thing during the night except beat up and down waiting for morning. Captain Tranter had not been called. Fox wondered if the captain of *Epernave* had been called, and if he had called Commodore Sharp. He wondered who had been the officer of the watch aboard the frigate. Then he turned away from that sightless staring at the beach where English soldiers had been left stranded. Wondering would help no one, not now.

If anyone aboard any of the ships of the flotilla was surprised when they nosed in to the beach to find it deserted of life then that one was a bloody fool in Fox's estimation.

Did they think the French would spend all night tucked up in bed when there were enemies of the Republic tramping their homeland?

A boat was sent from *Epernave*. From seaweed-covered rocks, a sergeant, a boy drummer and two privates crept out, their red uniforms sodden rags, their gaiters and boots in tatters, all their finery bedraggled. But the sergeant still had his spontoon and the soldiers their muskets, and the boy clutched his drum with its brave golden lettering with the clutch of desperate resolve.

Fox felt sick.

So that was it, then. He looked up to the rank grass of the heights above the beach. Cavalry pirouetted there. He caught the watery morning gleam of sunshine reflecting from cuirasses and helmets, from sabres and stirrups. He knew what the British force was doing now. They were marching away to captivity, to one of those cancerous prisons like Verdun or

Valincent. He knew without thought that the English redcoats had fought; but General Folsham would not wish to throw away his men's lives, a thousand of them, fighting a whole continent in arms.

Signal flags broke from the flagship. *Sheridan* got under way. *Epernave* would escort the force back to Margate; Sheridan would rejoin Sir Blundesely Creighton. Then Fox's lips fought to curl in contempt; but he could not in all honesty feel that full-blooded contempt for these aristocratic bunglers as he saw the boats with the flags of truce putting out from *Epernave* and the transports. He knew what they were doing. They would be taking the officers' baggage out, their comforts, making arrangements for letters to be written and lists of dead and wounded made up so that relatives in England might know the worst or the next-to-worst. No doubt arrangements for exchange for some of the French prisoners in English hands would even now be under way. Fox felt gagged. He could not condemn all this. But he could feel that slow-fire of resentment burning harshly-banked in him that it was the officers who received this treatment. He knew from his own experiences in America how the British soldier was treated.

Supposing his brother Bert had been among those captured men? The warm memories of Captain Rupert Colburn of the Forty Third Foot he always cherished and which he supposed were the nearest sentiments to friendship for another man he could entertain rose again in his mind. Rupert had taken young Bert under his wing. That knowledge pleased Fox. But supposing they were sent into action under incompetents? Supposing they were thrown away as those men had been discarded on the beach at Banquarie?

The planners of this irresponsible operation should have known that in any kind of cross-wind the beach would be impossible for boats. They should have known that, and they should have taken it into consideration. The ships had found no

53

inconvenience whatsoever at sea; it was the wind and the tide setting at right-angles that had caused the trouble — and those doddering old fools at the Admiralty should have known.

As was Fox's custom during any period of enforced imprisonment or restraint, he structured the time in terms of affairs. Counting in the time he'd spent on the lower deck of *Tiger* before those gold-laced idiots had realised he was an officer, there had been altogether too many affairs just lately. In the short amount of time left him with Captain Tranter there was the affair of the water butts — although that was mere repetition of routine, and the affair of the corvette *L'Anime* which smashed herself to pieces on the rocks taking with her destruction any hope of prize money festering in George Abercrombie Fox's avaricious brain.

Various plans had fermented in Fox's feverish brain and deflated themselves with puffs of hot air. A weak spot of the mad captain had to be found and exploited. He began to doubt that he could manage the plot he thought of in something akin to desperation. He, a loner, would need accomplices.

He cheered himself with the reflection that the madder the plot the better for dealing with a mad captain. Tranter was by no means mad all the time. Riddled by fear and unease and despair as his ship was, yet he kept her taught, able to lie in the line, the men exercised and ready. Then he would break out, dress in all his finery, sit on a chair on his quarterdeck with one foot nonchalantly resting on the bent back of his black servant Hannibal, smoking cigars and overseeing various punishments. The boatswain's mates had no liking for this kind of torture; but they knew well enough under the laws of the sea and the Admiralty that if they refused they would suffer the same indignities.

One main topman fell off the main topgallant yard and hit the sea head first. When they fished him out, blood poured from his nostrils and ears and he died within the hour.

"D.D."- Discharged Dead — would appear against his name in the muster book; but no indication of how he had come to die would be entered. The poor devil had been up on the topgallant yard feeding Tranter's imaginary pigeons until he grew faint.

Days melted into days, grew into weeks, fathomed out into fortnights and months, and towards the end of May *Sheridan,* with other units of the Channel Fleet, was ordered south, to join Earl Saint Vincent, commander-in-chief of the Mediterranean Fleet at present ignominiously turned out of the Inland Sea by the French and Spanish and engaged on the blockade of Cadiz.

A real and profound sense of excitement and anticipation uplifted the entire ship's company. Fox, despite his own pleasure at once more rejoining the Mediterranean Fleet, had his reservations. This could so easily be more days and weeks and months of blockade, the only difference being they would be beating off and on Cadiz.

Orders came down for the ship to be painted in Sir John's colours, black and yellow chequer-board, and the simple act of seeing that done brought back a flood of memories to Fox. That night he decided to open the first shot in his campaign.

Earl Saint Vincent was notorious as a strict disciplinarian, and he had a short way with mutineers. In the affair of the flicker of mutiny aboard *Marlborough* when the captain of that ship reported that his crew would not permit one of their number to be hung for mutiny, St. Vincent said: "Do you mean to tell me, Captain Elision that you cannot command His Majesty's ship *Marlborough?* If that is the case, sir, I will immediately send on board an officer who can. That man shall be hanged at eight o'clock tomorrow morning and by his own ship's company, for not a hand from any other ship in the Fleet shall touch the rope."

And next morning, as armed launches surrounded the *Marlborough,* his shipmates strung up the mutineer.

Earl Saint Vincent was not a man to be trifled with. He abominated slack captains and officers, and this was the only trump card Fox had. Fox would have to sail very warily, very warily, indeed, sounding all the way.

Chapter Six

As a boy Fox had spent many happy hours on the Thames marshes hunting wildfowl. He had used a sling and had become a superb marksman, an aptitude which now extended to his uncanny accuracy with guns of all kinds. He habitually carried with him a neatly folded black kerchief. That evening as the sky burned crimson all across the Atlantic horizon he carefully shook out the kerchief, folded it into a triangle and looped the ends between finger and thumb, cunningly. A pistol ball was carefully lodged in the fold, and Fox, out of view of Frobisher on the quarterdeck, took swift confident aim at the gull flitting over his head, slung, saw the bullet strike and the gull come fluttering down.

He retrieved it in the shadows and carried it forward to the galley where the captain's personal servant acting as his cook waited.

"You understand, Cookie, what you have to do?"

"Oh, aye, sir. I don't envy —" Then the man stopped, the realisation that he was not speaking to the captain, in whose good books he was perhaps the only man aboard, making him tongue-tied and awkward.

"Just make it look nice, Cookie." Fox spoke with a deliberateness he was aware might later on be used as evidence at his court martial. "I think the captain is entitled to the best diet we can manage for him."

He went out quickly from the galley before any more could be said that might serve to incriminate him. What he had done so far was unorthodox; but looking after his captain's creature comforts was no crime. He was pretty confident about that, although willing to allow that anything at all could be a crime in this man's navy if the high and mighty big-wigs so decided.

Unlike Captain bloody Sir bloody John bloody Pulteney — as Kitty used to describe him — Captain Tranter did deign to invite Fox to supper with him in his aft cabin. With Frobisher taking the first watch, from eight 'till midnight, Fox, the second lieutenant, a silent Scot, Mr. Frazer, and Mr. Midshipman Blount, shared the captain's bounty.

Cards were occasionally played; but Fox had no interest in cheating his comrades, even mad Captain Tranter, and the games came out around even.

This evening the talk was all on the prospects ahead, and of what Earl St Vincent had in store. "Mark my words," Tranter said, as sane as the next man as he spoke, "Old Jarvie is going back into the Med. We'll show those Dons and Frogs a lesson they won't forget."

The news had come that Nelson with Captains Saumarez and Ball, respectively in *Vanguard, Orion* and *Alexander,* all seventy fours, accompanied by three frigates, had been sent into the Med to scout Toulon. This upstart Napleone Buonaparte had collected a vast fleet there and no one had the slightest idea where the armament was intended to sail. For Fox, the most immediately pressing concern was the bird the messman was bringing in. After that he could begin to think about world-wide politics and high strategy.

58

"The enemy regard the Med as their own private boating lake," Mr. Frazer was saying, rolling his r's, and for him uttering a long speech, "I dinna gie' much for their chances when Nelson gets at 'em."

Nelson was a rear-admiral now, a knight of the Bath: but he had lost an arm as well as his eye. At least, Fox could give thanks he still had both arms and legs, even if his left eye mutinied on him during times of danger, stress or passion, and his right eye would hoist the skull-and-cross bones if he did not by the utmost effort of will keep it open and seeing for him. And Nelson was only seven years older than Fox, to the day, as they both shared the same birthday, 29th September.

George Abercrombie Fox was a humble lieutenant, without even a sword of honour and scratching around for all the prize money that might come his way, whilst Horatio Nelson was a rear-admiral, a knight, feted and honoured wherever he went and commanding a nucleus of a fleet that could win renown not only for England but for Nelson himself. Nelson was concerned with high strategy, with what Buonaparte would do, with three-deckers and seventy-fours, with politics and with admirals; Fox was concerned with a roast bird being placed on its silver salver before his mad captain.

Hannibal lifted the silver cover. Fox watched his captain with a rigid scrutiny. Tranter picked up the carving knife and fork, poised them, leant forward with the glutton's anticipatory smile on his face — and froze.

He stared at the roast bird.

His voice rose into a squeak.

"What's this?"

The other looked politely interested. Strongly, without hesitation, Fox said: "I felt you would like an addition to your diet, sir. A bird seemed indicated. I do trust you will find it to your liking."

Tranter lifted those curious red-rimmed eyes and regarded Fox across the table. The lantern swinging above their heads, the heave and surge of the ship, the eternal creak of woodwork and the wind in the rigging thrumming through the timbers of the ship from the chains resolved into a noisy tableau in which Tranter and Fox stared at each other over the steaming carcass of a bird on a silver platter.

"It's pigeon!" screamed Tranter. "One of my pigeons!"

"Pigeon, sir?"

"Curse you for a black Jacobin bastard! Pigeon I said!" Tranter thrust the carving knife out stiffly, and the lantern light ran in runnels of liquid fire from its edge. "Pigeon, sir! That's what this is. D'you think I don't know one of my own pigeons when I see one?"

Frazer and Blount had the sense to remain absolutely still and silent. Fox put on that bewildered air he could fashion up in his ugly features.

"I'm afraid I don't follow you, sir. That is a gull —"

"Gull! D'you think I'm a simpleton, sir? Gull! *Gull!*"

"Yes, sir." Then Fox went smoothly on. "A gull, sir."

The knife and fork crashed down on the swinging table. Tranter staggered up, knocking wine glasses to the deck. He was gobbling with fury now, waving his arms, strangling with the passion surging in him.

"It's pigeon, sir — pigeon! And I recognise her — my Annabell, the sweetest little flyer of my whole family! I'll have you court-martialled, sir! Dismissed the service! A thousand lashes! Life imprisonment — I'll have you dangling from the main yardarm before sun-up, so help me!"

Fox kept his breathing steady. Some of the threats Tranter had uttered he could do. Fox knew that.

"It is gull, sir, arranged by me as a special treat for you. I can only protest ignorance of any pigeon." He breathed in, watching Tranter, and then said flatly: "After all, who heard of pigeons on board a ship six months at sea?"

Blount made a strange weaselly sniffling sound. Frazer remained as still and silent as a mummy in a pyramid. Hannibal dropped the silver cover with a clatter that no one noticed.

Tranter suddenly clutched his throat. His eyes protruded in his head. He opened his mouth and fought for breath. Impatiently, Fox thought to himself: "Why doesn't the old fool fall down?" The man was going to have a fit. Well then, Fox considered, let him have the decency to get it over with as soon as possible.

He waited a moment, and then said: "If you wish to have me court-martialled, sir, Lord Saint Vincent's flagship is a couple of cables' lengths off. I think he would be delighted to use his well-known disciplinary strictness upon an officer who goes to great lengths to provide his captain with delicacies for the table and is then accused in the most unwarrantably false fashion —"

He halted there, deliberately. Tranter was making movements in the air with his left hand, gobbling with his mouth, his tongue was curled out, his eyes enormous and bulging. But still he did not fall down.

Fox said to Hannibal: "Run on deck, my compliments to Mr. Frobisher, and will he kindly step down here for a moment." As Hannibal reached the door, Fox added, speaking directly at Tranter: "It is clear that our captain is unfit to continue in his duty. Mr. Frobisher will have to assume command and send a signal to the flagship to that effect. I trust you gentlemen concur?"

Neither Blount nor Frazer would trust themselves or the moment to reply.

When Frobisher bundled angrily into the cabin, forewarned by Hannibal's manner that something was amiss, Tranter had still not recovered or fallen. He stood, choking, trying to speak, his head jutting further and further upwards so that his bulging eyes floated on fat red rims.

Before Frobisher could speak, Fox said: "Mr. Frobisher. You see the condition of Captain Tranter. He is — unwell. We must all proceed with the utmost caution. If you decide to assume command and so inform his lordship I will give you my full support."

Frobisher was thus presented with a case flung in his face. He stared in fascinated horror at Tranter. The captain made a supreme effort. His rigid jaw muscles writhed. His mouth half-closed. His breath rasped like chains through a hawse-hole. He forced breath between his teeth.

"Pigeons —" said Captain Tranter.

Then he fell. He fell full length, unbending, rigid, and his head struck the swinging corner of the table and bright blood poured out and he rolled over to finish up against the bulkhead, unconscious.

By the time Hannibal had the captain tucked into his cot and the surgeon had begun to get his implements ready to bleed him, Fox had managed to bring Frobisher on to the right tack.

"If you so decide, sir," he said as though it was a matter for Frobisher's decision. "I will go over to the flagship and make a full report. It would be better for me to go, as the unwitting cause of the captain's final collapse. We all, I think, gentlemen, are aware of the true nature of this malady." In view of the time of evening and the distance a cutter was hoisted out and Fox, taking with him Midshipman Blount as further corroborative evidence, pushed off for the flagship. He knew there was no question of Frobisher assuming command.

Not when a full admiral sailed a couple of cables' length off, and that admiral was John Jervis, old Jarvie, the most noted disciplinarian in the Navy.

The interview was short. Sir John — Earl St Vincent now, Fox corrected himself — had changed since they had last met. He had grown older and greyer; but that sharp intellectual look in his eyes, that curve to his lips, almost sneering in their effect, remained the same. Looking into that face Fox was well aware how many men had stood where he stood looking into that face and shuddered to their souls. How many floggings, how many hangings, had this man ordered?

"It is no surprise to me." St Vincent said. "Fox, Fox? Weren't you in that affair with *Daffodil?*"

"Yes, sir," said Fox, unsure whether to be pleased or frightened that Jerves remembered him.

"Hm. We don't want to make a cause célèbre out of this affair. You did right to come personally and report. I'll see to it. I have enough ambitious young lieutenants wanting to be posted. You may go."

"Thank you, sir." Fox followed his usual custom. He had made up his mind, calculated out the odds like any gambler, and, short of a change in circumstances would follow through his plan without hesitation. "I am still borne on the books of *Duchess,* sir. I was in *Sheridan* only on a temporary supernumerary understanding."

"Well?"

"*Sheridan* has her full complement of officers, sir. With your lordships' permission I would like you to authorise my transfer to *Culloden.*"

The admiral stuck his head down, his lips thinning in the complicated curve, his eyes bright like a vulture's upon Fox. "You know Captain Troubridge?"

"I have no influence whatsoever in the navy, sir. But I believe Captain Troubridge to be —" He stopped. Then, annoyed that he had betrayed a weakness, he added: "I would be happy to be posted to any appointment your lordship feels suitable."

"You're a spirited one, and I remember about *Daffodil* now. "I believe you know my views on officers who do not obey their orders? I see. As it happens, Captain Troubridge is sailing with special instructions. I think he would welcome another officer where he is going. We're all shorthanded enough as it is."

Fox dared to breathe again. He could not believe that St Vincent had any feelings of pity for so old a man who was so recently promoted to lieutenant after a near-lifetime's hitch as a midshipman. If St Vincent cared to remember even further back he might recall Fox as a ship's boy; and Fox was not at all sure that would help his case now.

"Mr. Fox — Fox — yes." St. Vincent hunched his hands into the small of his back. All those officers seemed to do that. "Sir Blundesely mentioned in a letter something about a Fox being in a devilish funny situation aboard *Tiger* — ?"

Fox nodded. "Yes, sir. That was me."

St Vincent made up his mind. There are no powers in the whole world so awful as those of a full admiral flying his flag at sea. Even Kings and prime ministers and archbishops are fettered in comparison.

"You'll need to return to *Sheridan* to pick up your baggage. I'll have orders written for Captain Troubridge."

Fox let himself perform that silly ha harrumph.

"I have my gear in the cutter, sir."

St. Vincent rounded on him, hesitated, and then nodded curtly to indicate the interview was over. Going out, Fox let his breath out again. He seemed forever hanging on to his breath as though each one was his last.

Midshipman Blount, who had remained on the quarterdeck and had not been asked to give evidence, opened his mouth in astonishment when Fox jumped in beside him on the sternsheets of the cutter and told the crew to give way — and then headed for *Culloden.*

"Give Mr. Frobisher my compliments, Mr. Blount," was all that Fox would say. Then he relented. "Tell him that I sincerely trust his next captain will be more to his liking."

"Yes, sir," said Blount. He spoke as one delivered from lions. "I'll tell him that." The weasel face looked less long and lugubrious now. Perhaps, Fox wondered, knowing with a vast sense of relief that it no longer concerned him, just perhaps *Sheridan* might turn out to be a happy ship now.

Then he was scrambling up the side of *Culloden* and all the future was changed.

Chapter Seven

His lungs could expand now, the weight was gone from his chest, the tightened band around his forehead had been loosened. Even his experiences aboard *Tiger* when he had had a knock about the head and was sick and dizzy, faded in comparison with the tightrope over disaster that had been every single hour in *Sheridan*. Captain Troubridge welcomed him in kindly fashion. The spirit aboard *Culloden* was something new and yet familiar to Fox. These were the men, this the ship, that with others of like mettle had licked the Spanish at St Vincent last year. What had Jervis — as he was then — said as *Culloden* led the line into action? "Look at Troubridge! He handles his ship as if the eyes of all England were upon him!"

During the abortive attack on Santa Cruz when Nelson lost his arm, Troubridge had captured the mole, driven into the piazza with his four hundred men — then their ammunition had run out. So fierce was the fighting determination of Troubridge and his men that the Spanish Governor of Santa Cruz had thought it advisable to parley with them before they destroyed everything, and, acting well, arranged a parley and provided them with boats and food and wine for their departure. That made Fox smile, in his grim, never-smiling fashion.

Now he could surface to life after the constriction of *Sheridan,* he realised that all was not well for England. He had known it before, now he understood why the country looked to the Navy, why men like St Vincent, and Howe, and Duncan and, even, Nelson, were regarded with near-idolatry. England expected invasion; the little pinpricks of raids like that in which he had participated at Banquarie would not stop the French once they made up their minds. Austria's surrender had surrendered the continent. Ireland was in ferment — Fox felt a deep sense of loss over that unhappy island. Robert Colburn had written long intimate letters that Fox found himself reading and re-reading; and Rupert hinted that the divisions were less those between Protestant and Roman Catholic than between aristocrat and landed absentee gentry and the poor, the peasants, the oppressed. If only the damned French hadn't stuck their long, unwanted noses in.

Everyone surmised that the immense armada this Corsican bandit Bonaparte — he had changed the spelling of his name — was assembling at Toulon was intended for Ireland.

Lord Spencer at the Admiralty must be playing long odds to risk sending a Fleet of thirteen ships of the line and one fifty gun ship into the Med at a time when all England's resources should have been scraped together to ward off the hammer blow of invasion and the anvil of Irish rebellion. St Vincent had shown iron integrity of purpose when he detached his best ships, his inshore squadron, to sail with Nelson. Those storm-beaten ships, lean and hungry for action, dogs of war, would rend and savage the slack Revolutionary ships of France — if they could find them.

Nelson in *Vanguard* had repaired his storm-shattered topmasts and on 6th June he was found by Troubridge. His orders were simple. He was to find and destroy the French Fleet — for that formidable armament had sailed when Nelson's eyes, his frigates, had been forced to return to Gibraltar. Anywhere in the world, in theory, could that French Fleet have sailed with Bonaparte aboard.

Fox settled down with pleasant ease aboard this new ship of his, and bearing in mind that, as far as he was concerned he was still borne on the books of *Duchess* — wherever she might be now — he could not refrain from wondering for how long he would be left aboard *Culloden.*

They sailed past the Genoese Riviera and along the Italian coast. When they sighted topmasts in a flock over the horizon, Fox rubbed his hands. That was a Spanish merchant convoy, still believing that the Mediterranean was their private lake, and Fox began to estimate what his share of the prize money would be.

"We could be rich for life in three hours!" commented a midshipman to his friend, staring through their telescopes at that fat and luscious prey.

Moments passed, the British line continued, no signal flags for a change of course floated to the rear-admirals yardarm. The ships drew away from the Spanish. Fox cursed. Glory and honour — that was all anyone thought about now, in this moment of England's peril. The two middies sensed that.

"The admiral can't stop for fat Spanish prizes now," said one, knowingly. "It's the French for him!"

"Aye, and for us. Sink me if we don't sink every one of them!"

Privately Fox could mouth his disappointment, openly he must share the general eagerness for action with the French, to smash this great armada that sought to rouse all Ireland against England. When action did come there would be opportunity for prize money. He felt supremely confident of that. With an officer like Nelson in command and with ships like those around him, no fleet in the world could stand against them.

On the 14th June, news was taken from a passing vessel that Bonaparte's fleet had been sighted — but to the west of Sicily. Rumours swept the ship. Admitted strong westerly winds were blowing, making it difficult for the lubberly French to pass the Gut; but still and all there were more things in the wind than signal pendants. By the 17th, Naples was in sight and there was much coming and going from the shore. Fox stared at this most beautiful of cities and beat down the longing that rose in him. His mind turned instinctively to Kitty. How he missed those white arms, those soft lips, her hoarse honeyed voice!

Bonaparte, it seemed, had taken Malta.

Then the bombshell burst. Fox expressed the same surprise as everyone else, until calm reasoning superseded wild surmise. Bonaparte was going to Egypt. No proof existed. But when they heard that Nelson believed this, had divined it, the lower deck, at least, believed. The ships crowded all sail for Alexandria. Fox spent his time looking across the blue sea, longing for the sight of the French line-of-battleships. He hungered for action to bring in the prize money he so desperately needed for his family.

French frigate topsails were sighted; but Nelson ignored them. He was after the big ones, the transports, the seventy-fours. "If only we had some frigates!" Fox said, bitterly. It could be a decisive moment was slipping away ..

Driving on in a nervous suspense, the English fleet at last reached Alexandria. Fox knew he mirrored everyone's feelings when he saw the roadstead empty. No French! He felt as though everything had gone wrong. Despite all his cynical feelings about admirals this Nelson was different from the rest — and Nelson had been wrong! Nelson had failed!

The fleet span about and headed away to the north east on the 29th, dropping the Pharos tower astern.

Now a sullen vengeful feeling grew. The French must be somewhere in this Inland Sea — the thought that they had doubled back, had slipped through the Straits, were out on the open Atlantic, tortured the English. St Vincent was there. He would stop them. He would have to! All England and Ireland lay open. Fox felt to the very roots of his being that he was living through days of monumental history; that everything said and done in these days would find an immortal niche in the history of the world.

Fox could guess what the reactions in St Vincent's fleet off Cadiz and among the bigwigs in England would be. Nelson was too young, they'd cry. Admirals would resign in pique at being passed over. There would be a hullabaloo for Nelson's recall. Fox had no love for admirals and authority in any form; but he had seen Nelson's Fleet and he knew the man; he'd go with Nelson against the devil himself, if he had to, and there was prize money in it. As for the honour and glory that Nelson so hungered for, Fox allowed that was his weakness, magnanimously.

The middies were forever singing silly tunes from Thomas Dibdin's play *The British Raft,* which had, so Fox understood, been first performed on Easter Monday last year at Sadler's Wells. Rupert wrote him scathing accounts of the foppish dress of the Volunteers and confided that with all their scarlet coats, and multicoloured facings, and gold lace and feathers, they had precious few muskets between them. Bonaparte's veterans of Italy, Fox guessed, would make short work of the Volunteers. And that formidable army was on the high seas — somewhere — and Nelson had not found either the army or the Fleet.

The water was almost all gone; foul and slimy with green growing things, it was an abomination. They put in on 19th July at Syracuse in Sicily where the authorities, frightened to incur the wrath of the French colossus, would have stood on

71

their rights as neutrals and refused help to the British squadron, allowing only four ships in at a time. Fox heard of the way Nelson got over that one. He wrote not to the British Ambassador at Naples, as one might have thought, to make representations to His Majesty King Ferdinand; instead he wrote to the Ambassador's wife, Emma, to use her influence with the Queen, Maria Carolina. The Sicilians received the order to victual and water the English ships in secret, so as not to draw down thunderbolts of anger from France, and the seamen's watering parties filled their butts and barrels and kegs at the fountain of Arethusa.

That made Fox wonder, did that.

Sailing in three closed-up divisions ready for immediate action the moment the enemy's topsails showed they left for the Morea on 25th. The idea was for two divisions to grapple with and destroy the French line-of-battle ships whilst the third division dealt with the storeships and transports.

Captain Troubridge would go aboard *Vanguard* whenever the weather allowed. Fox never failed to notice the reanimation when the captain returned, as though something was taking place on the quarterdeck of *Vanguard* with Nelson that had the effect of creating a living flame of purpose among every single man and boy of the Fleet. He could not remain immune to that brand. All preparations were made. Everyone knew what they had to do. When the battle was joined all the long preparation and waiting would be over and they could fling themselves into the smoke and flame of action secure in the knowledge that they were the finest fighting force the seas had ever seen.

The ships themselves sounded like a roll call to fame and glory.

There were *Culloden; Orion* commanded by that saturnine man, Saumarez; *Thesus* that Captain Miller had turned from a hellship into one of the best afloat; *Swiftsure* commanded by the Canadian Hallowell, *Bellerophon; Defence; Minotaur,* Captain Louis; *Zealous,* Captain Hood with the notable relations; *Goliath,* Tom Foley; *Majestic; Alexander,* Captain Alexander Ball who had towed Nelson to safety; *Audacious;* the small fifty gun ship *Leander;* and, leading the whole Fleet, *Vanguard,* commanded by Captain Edward Berry, the first man into the mizzen-chains of the *Saint Nicholas.*

They were, indeed, even to Fox, a very fine company of ships.

Then Troubridge found news in the Gulf of Coron that a Fleet had been sighted a month earlier leaving Crete and heading south eastward.

Egypt! It could only be Egypt. So Nelson had been right after all. Fox calculated out what had happened and came to the conclusion that the two Fleets must somehow have crossed tracks and missed each other. It must have been a close shave. Bonaparte would have come to grief then, surely.

The men, the ships, the officers, the guns, all were ready. In this tenacious pursuit, a honed edge had been put on the Fleet. Constant exercises — with the guns, with the small arms — a minute attention to every detail, marked that far-flung and incredibly dogged persistence in the hunt. Everyone was keyed up. The French *must* be in Egypt!

The lookouts called down as the Pharos' tower hove in sight on the 1st August. The congregation, assembled to search the roads, stared with eager anticipation. But only the masts of merchantmen showed as the afternoon wore on. Nothing! No French Fleet! No Admiral Brueys!

Fox cursed with the others. A dull feeling of resignation settled. *Culloden* had picked up a small prize and was towing her and so had dropped a little astern of the main Fleet, and *Swiftsure* and *Alexander* were off making a closer inspection of Alexandria. The Fleet bore away to the eastward, as they had done before, and the frustration and futile rage seemed to coalesce in a dun cloud above their mastheads.

The afternoon wore on and the Fleet sailed on. Fox found himself wondering what were the thoughts running through Admiral Nelson's mind. What now of the quest for glory and honour? More to the point, what of Fox's insensate desire for prize money?

Primed, trembling for action, ready to burst with all the vigour of which they were capable, the English Fleet sailed along the coast from Alexandria. Fox watched their sails ahead of him as the light died. Those sails were all set and straining. They were vanishing beyond the point of land jutting out seawards. Something caught at Fox then, some zephyr of an excitement he could never afterwards explain.

Then came the first rolling thunders of guns being fired.

At once, Fox made himself scarce. If Troubridge cast off the prize, Fox had no desire at all, the very last thing in the world, to be nominated to take over her command. Up ahead he could hear the broadsides crashing out. They had done it! Nelson had found the French!

In the thickening dark now, they could see the reflected flashes and flames lighting up the sky. The sounds of battle rolled across the sea towards them. Every stitch of canvas was drawing. Rightfully, *Culloden* was regarded as the finest ship in the English Fleet, here entering a battle that would decide the domination of the Mediterranean. Fox had no doubts whatsoever that the English would win; he had no doubts that he would personally live through the battle; his main considerations were the amounts of prize money he could claim after the victory.

Now they were rounding the headland where mortars were firing ineffectually at them. The whole bay — it was the bay of Aboukir, so the charts said — was lit up. Smoke rolled in dense masses. *Culloden,* showing her teeth, swept on. The

French had anchored in a long curving line very close up to the shore, thirteen line-of-battle ships, with what looked like a second line of frigates shorewards of them.

"Look!" Troubridge pointed. "That's Foley — he's rounded the head of their line and anchored shorewards of them! And Hood — and Saumarez!"

"*Minotaur, Bellerophon* and *Majestic* are outside, sir!" said the first lieutenant, joy all over his face. "We've got them between a nutcracker!"

It was clear that the French had anchored in what they had considered a formidable place of defence with only their starboard sides exposed, and the English had coolly sailed in over the shallows, around their head, and were now crashing broadsides into them from both directions. Beyond the van the rest of the line lay half-concealed in smoke and the darkness that followed as the sun sank in sheets and floods of gold and crimson. The night was lit as brightly as ever Fox could remember; he felt sure at least one ship was on fire. The noise rolled up to them against the wind, which blew from the northwest. Troubridge was staring ahead, with all the hunger for action that had consumed them all over the harrowing weeks of the chase, making his face into a blazing fire-illuminated gargoyle. Fox knew they all looked like that.

In bare moments they would be entering the inferno. The men stood to their guns, their black kerchiefs tied around their foreheads, stripped to the waist. The marines lined the rail. The ship's boys were ready to scamper up from the magazines with powder. Water-soaked sand strewed the decks. The yards had been double-slung; everything was ready. A heady excitement that Fox distrusted gripped him; but his right eye remained cool and he had no premonition of its treacherous abandonment of duty.

Steadily *Culloden* stood on into the battle.

Following in her wake sailed *Swiftsure* and *Alexander*.

"By the way they're going at it hammer and tongs," said a voice from the quarterdeck, "it could be all over before we arrive up."

"Pray heaven it isn't so," answered another voice. They were all standing staring forward, the firelight on their faces, the sounds of battle in their ears.

They had rounded the island by now. The leadsman in the chains was singing out the soundings. The night sky, the rush of water, the spring and rhythm of the ship, the cataclysmic battle ahead of them, all merged in Fox's senses. This was the feel of a great Fleet action. He suddenly realised he wouldn't want to be anywhere else in the whole world, and called himself, with great contempt, a stupid fool for being caught up in emotional claptrap. He fingered the cutlass he had taken up, his own captured Spanish sword being still aboard *Duchess.* He'd use that this night, bigod! Use it to knock a few French heads in. He felt no elation at the thought, only a continuation of the desire shared by the whole Fleet and certainly by the *Culloden,* the finest ship in that Fleet, to get in at the enemy and do the job they had thirsted for so long to do.

The four white lights suspended from the mizzen-peak marked the British ships; in all that inferno of fire and smoke which together created a scene of incredible grandeur and lofty sentiment, and which cloaked, as Fox well knew, scenes of unparalleled horror, the hour of decision had come.

In only a few more moments he would be plunged into that cauldron of fire and in the storms of grapeshot and langrage and round shot, and the hail of musketry, he would once more risk his life for the pay a grateful country allowed him and the prize money he could earn.

The men were cheering as fires belched up ahead. The leadsman was singing out the soundings and heaving the lead with as much nonchalance as though negotiating some tranquil bay at home. He called out the depth at eleven fathoms which was ample water in which to pass the island and began to coil his line ready for the next heave.

Fox fingered his cutlass hilt again. Not long now. Streamers of fire reflected in the water pointed long fingers at him, as though beckoning him into the mouth of hell. The officers on the quarterdeck were talking, a few were laughing, some were clearly letting their tensions take control. But everywhere that dominant spirit of getting into the fight prevailed. This time they'd get in among the enemy and show

—

Culloden thumped from ahead. Everybody staggered. She had lost way. Water slapped at her sides in a frightening way, in the fashion of dead water. She stopped. The leadsman hurled his line; but Fox knew that was a waste of time. A bestial growl rose from the ship. Troubridge — Fox couldn't bear to look on Troubridge in that instant.

A voice, guttural, hoarse, disbelieving, screamed:
"We're aground!"

Chapter Eight

George Abercrombie Fox had never known a birthday like it.

The twenty-ninth of September, 1798, his thirty-third birthday, was celebrated in a style at once crazy, magnificent, lavish and overwhelming. The whole of Naples went mad. Massive displays of fireworks festooned the soft night air with crackling discharges, and colours, and fizzing glories of pyrotechnical wizardry. A grand Dinner was held at the Ambassador's, Sir William Hamilton's, and although Fox did not attend, he was most certainly present at the enormous ball to which the monstrous total of one thousand seven hundred and forty people came to dance the night away. Eight hundred people were served supper. George Abercrombie Fox never really had celebrated his birthday like this before.

The signorinas with their bright eyes and curling oily black hair and swarthy complexions were ecstatic at the sight of any man in British naval uniform. Wine flowed, clustered candles and magnificent candelabra blazed, footmen glided swiftly bearing trays of goodies, the music festooned gay tunes through the overheated air. Faces shone with delight as sweat trickled through caked powder, men and women danced and pranced and grew breathless, and laughed, and drank toast after toast to the hero of the hour.

Yes, it really was a birthday to remember.

Fox planned his night's operations with his usual meticulous attention to detail. First, he would not drink so much he fell about incapable. Second, he would gorge enough of the lavish food to last him, in memory, through the times when he would be living on salt pork and weevilly biscuits and scummy water. Third, he would find a cosy little party of these rich Neapolitan lords playing cards, and make enough money to turn the whole affair into a more profitable business deal for him and the family. And, fourth and last, he would find himself one of these cuddly Neapolitan signorinas and — well, let nature take its disgusting course.

The people kept cheering the hero of the hour, and drinking toasts to him. Buttons and ribbons bore his name everywhere, they'd even added a verse about him and the Battle of the Nile, as it was being called, to the National Anthem. That the name thus apostrophised and blazed forth in fireworks and dinner plates, was Nelson, and not Fox, was just another example of the inequity between a humble lieutenant, born a Thames marsh-boy without influence, and a rear-admiral — soon to be of the red — with the world at his feet, who had been a post captain before he was twenty-one.

A memory Fox took away with him was of a brief meeting with Sir William's wife, Emma, a woman with a sweet full face, a plump and delightful figure — Fox had heard all about the "attitudes" — and a sense of almost tomboyish eagerness and vivacity, a woman all through, alive and living life to the hilt, at the moment on top of the world, worshipping Nelson, and, not so oddly considering their respective circumstances, reminded of Kitty. Not with all these pliant Neapolitan girls thronging around the blue and white of the navy. Fox had been brought to Naples in his capacity as a supernumerary, leaving *Culloden* and the tragic figure of Troubridge. There was grim work for all the Fleet on the morrow.

As for *Culloden* — had Fox been of a lachrymose character he would have wept. There they'd been, sweeping into the bay of Aboukir, the French fleet before them engaged with Nelson's Fleet, the thunder of the broadsides in their ears, the flash and roar of combat thrilling through their blood, a few hundred yards to go to join that immortal band who were destroying Bonaparte's' naval power in the eastern Mediterranean — and ignominiously they had stuck fast on a sandbank.

Troubridge had gone near-insane. Fox just couldn't bring himself to recall how the captain had taken this mortal blow. For mortal it was, if not in the physical sense then in the career sense; everyone sung Troubridge's praises, acknowledging his personal bravery, and giving him credit for his grounded ship acting as a warning beacon so that *Swiftsure* and *Alexander,* seeing her stuck, could swing safely past that treacherous shoal. Commander Hardy in the brig *Mutine* had come alongside with offers of help. The men's cursing had blistered the night air as much, it seemed, as the cannonading going on so near. Nothing would get the ship off. All that night as Bonaparte's Fleet was destroyed or taken, with the two exceptions of *Guillaume-Tell* and *Genereux* of the line, and a couple of frigates, the men had fought their guns and then slumped exhausted, only to rear up and fight on. When the French flagship, *Orient,* with Admiral Brueys on board, blew up, the detonation was the largest that many people had ever witnessed. For a few moments afterwards, not a gun spoke, and silence wrapped the appalled fleets.

And the French had fought. Fox had never been one of those jaunty know-it-alls who claimed the Frogs could not fight. When the story of Captain Du Petit-Thouars, of *Tonnant,* became known, Fox was not surprised. Du Petit-Thouars had had both arms and a leg shot off and, bleeding to death, had had his body stood up in a barrel and had exhorted his men never to give up the fight. Only when *Tonnant* was aground and helpless were her colours struck on the 3rd.

Captain Thompson of *Leander,* who had tried to tow *Culloden* off, had been delayed into action because of that. As an irony of war, *Leander,* carrying Captain Berry with the Nile despatches, had been caught up with in a calm by one of the escaped French ships, *Genereux,* and after a protracted and unequal battle had been forced to strike. *Leander* had fifty guns and two hundred and eighty two men and boys. *Genereux* was a seventy four and carried no less than nine hundred and thirty six. A third of the *Leander's* crew were killed and wounded. After the action the French, so everyone said, treated the British abominably, which saddened Fox.

The more George Abercrombie Fox thought about his life and what he was doing on this earth the more he saw that, given the parameters, the events of his Battle of the Nile were inevitable. Of fourteen ships sailing down into battle, if one had to run aground and thus forfeit any chance of distinction for her officers and men, then our hero, as Fox ironically dubbed himself in moments of morbidity, would inevitably be aboard.

He tried to rouse himself. Everyone was acting as though world history had been altered. Well, maybe it had. He had a few drinks inside him, and he'd eaten until that stomach-bulge of which he was so conscious was protruding like a shy walrus looking out of a hole, and he was looking, without any shyness whatsoever, for the card players of Naples. He'd heard they were sharp.

They were. Their rapacious faces, partially illumined by the candles, their lean nervous hands, their glinting eyes, their rat-trap mouths, clearly indicated to Fox, as he joined the card party in a small side-room, that he had found his level. That his level might be in the gutter didn't worry him; he didn't give a damn what level he occupied provided it paid well.

These were the high-and-mighties of Naples. No *lazzaroni* would be admitted here, no peasants or farmers who cultivated the grape and the olive, who worked in the city, who fished in the sea, only those who were fair prey to Fox. But they were sharp. Very sharp. George Abercrombie Fox was just that bit smarter than they were, that was their trouble.

He walked out of the ornate gilt and ormolu and marble room feeling the gold jingling in its purse and feeling like having a chuckle at his winning, had he been the kind of man who chuckled that easily.

"Hey, *mistaire!*" She was attractive, her head on one side — thankfully with no rose between her teeth, indoors, that would have been bad taste — but her eyes were saucy enough and her dress transparent enough and her face not too swarthy for a man of Fox's fastidious tastes. He bowed. "Signorina?"

"Hey, *Inglese, Io sono molto —*" She dazzled him with her smile and linking arms manoeuvred him into a marble alcove. She shoved up against him, boldly. "I spik *Inglese* good, *si?* Good? Hey, *mistaire?*"

Fox made his mouth curve into the sort of smile this girl would expect. Routine could be allowed to take over now. He spoke in his Italian, which was not quite so good as his French or Spanish but which nevertheless was fluent and easy and idiomatic.

He'd sometimes cursed his powerful memory that enabled him to remain right on top of anything he really set his hand to; but it did mean he could ape accents and manners and pick up foreign tongues fluently. Ape, he often felt with a bitterness he had once vowed he would never let swamp him, ape was a good description of the way the aristocracy regarded the great mass of the people.

"Let's bear away for your snug little harbour, eh, my gal?"

She giggled, clinging to his arm, warm and soft and reasonably clean. Her musky female-odours were carrying out a spirited rear-guard action with the heavy scents with which she had deluged herself before the ball. As they proceeded under all plain sail they were attacked by a swarm of privateers intent on cutting out Fox, this fat prize, from the three-decker who had him in tow. Girls clawed at his new friend, spitting and shrieking, and masses of artificial hair toppled and tilted in the roseate light shed by candles and lanterns. She beat them back with her free hand, screaming out the most delightful Neapolitan abuse, which has a long and honourable history, rivalling that of the Thamesside where Fox had been reared up until he was ten years old. He ducked a white arm, felt a pair of soft lips squash against his cheek, caught the smell of female bodies pressing all about him, the rustle and flutter of dresses and petticoats, the sabre-like actions of feathers and fans. Then the three-decker towed her prize clear and they were running, laughing and skipping — at least, she was — up the broad marble staircase beneath the candelabra.

Ornately uniformed palace-guards stared blankly at them. She was a maid of the bed-chamber, or something similar — probably emptied the night-pot over the balcony and was paid a full captain's wages for doing it — and her name was Lucia and Fox was eager and ready to give up all the naval metaphors as they entered her room. A single candle burned. The bed was high and broad and extremely lumpy and, as soon as they were both fairly on it, a refuge of the most exciting and exquisite kind for Fox. As he said, coming up for air a half-an-hour later: "If all wars were like this there'd be no need of press gangs."

She let him out of her chamber the following morning. He felt satisfactorily fragile and hollow.

They had arranged to meet later on, for a walk in the gardens, and probably a stroll down to watch the ships of the Great Nelson at anchor. Fox remembered the seamen pent in those ships and frowned. If all captains were like Nelson, or Troubridge, or Collingwood, the men wouldn't mind too much. But, all captains were not like that dazzling band around Nelson; far too many of them were like poor old Tranter had been, or Grantley Struthers of *Duchess* on whose books Fox had gambled he still remained written down, or that toadying ninny Lord Lymm. Fox shrugged the displeasing memories off and about to see about breakfast was accosted by a large, lumpy, sweating and annoyed commander.

"Mr. Fox?"

"Yes, sir."

"It's damned lucky I had business with the admiral this morning and ran across you."

Fox set his face into its accustomed polite blankness.

"Lucky for you, Mr. Fox. You are appointed as my lieutenant. We sail in *Raccoon* this afternoon. You'd better cut along and see that all supplies necessary are aboard." The commander mopped his brow and swore. "It's the most infernal nuisance that old fool Macbridge going lame on me." Fox remained silent as the commander added, with a venom Fox understood and condemned: "Masters have no right aping the manners of their betters and getting thick heads as a consequence."

Fox had it all, now, all worked out nice and neatly. Despite his instant aversion to this swearing, bad-tempered incompetent, he felt that forbidden thrill of excitement lifting him. He would be *first* lieutenant ...

He decided to get things in perspective from the start. *Raccoon.* Yes, a brig brought in as a prize. So this would be Commander the honourable Cedric Mortlock. Fox took a breath.

"To whom," he said with a pricey quality about his inflexion, "have I the honour of addressing myself?"

Commander Mortlock turned his massive head to frown down on Fox. The man was a giant, a good six feet one. His eyes looked puzzled, he was genuinely amazed.

"Good God, man, don't you know who I am?"

Fox looked up calmly. "If I was in possession of your name, sir, I scarcely think it would be necessary to enquire."

Had he gone too far at the beginning?

"I'm Commander Mortlock, Fox. I was promoted into *Raccoon* from *L'Heroine*. My Master has gone sick on me and I'm told you have some aptitude at navigation."

Fox kept down the boiling rage. He was just a warrant officer's replacement. He said: "Mr. Fox, if you don't mind sir."

Mortlock opened his mouth, closed it, opened it again as his big face flushed crimson, caught sight of the look in Fox's eyes, and closed his mouth again, with a snap, as though he'd caught a fly.

"I'll trouble you to get down to *Raccoon* and do as I have ordered, Mr. Fox."

"Aye, aye, sir," said Fox. He rolled off. Let the big ape pick the bones out of that one. At the beginning Fox felt he had gained some measure of control. He'd read the signals aright, then. Just another aristocratic nincompoop, promoted through influence, requiring the constant services of a Master to enable him to run his ship. Although the *Raccoon* was a brig, not a ship.

And what a sweet vessel she was! Fox studied her as he was rowed out. He'd always had a fondness for the brig-rigged vessel; knowing how to get the best out of the two masts, cunningly handled, they could sail rings around a ship of the same size despite the absence of aft wind-leverage afforded by a mizzen. But in inexpert hands a brig became a sea-cow, unmanageable, intractable, a nightmare. He thought, for an instant, of the snow *Jolly Return,* and then shut that chapter away in the locked chambers of his mind.

There followed a period of hustle and bustle as he saw to the final preparations for sea. Most of the work had been done and, as was customary, the last items aboard were the water casks. Carker, the master's mate who would act as the third officer, seemed to Fox capable, level-headed and moulded in that tradition of sea-service that had for so long brought victory to the Royal Navy. The only midshipman aboard, although technically ranking as officer, was a mere boy of fourteen or so, called Johnny Prentiss and his services would be unreliable except in the most simple of sea evolutions.

Fox looked at the bay of Naples, Vesuvius spouting away, the white houses, the Castle of the Egg, the palace, imagining it all in his mind's eye as portions of the spectacle were hidden by ships or buildings, and he thought he'd had a good run ashore. He did not mind going back to sea too much. At least, he was a first lieutenant, even if only of a brig — and then he felt shame at the thought. *Raccoon* was a sweet craft.

She was French, of course. She measured about two hundred and twenty tons and she carried fourteen little four pounders on the broadsides, with a couple of long nines as bowchasers on the forecastle. Her rig was particularly lofty and reminded Fox of some he had seen in America. He'd have to make sure his topmen kept at the peak of fitness and efficiency to handle her. He'd keep 'em like that. The mates would use their colts to start the men, well-enough; but training was more than a question of flicking a sailor's backside. She carried ninety in her crew and Fox knew that most of them would be pleased — or as pleased as any seaman ever was — at the chance of getting out of their old ships and the prospects opening out before them aboard a small, fast ship which would be used — he fervently hoped and trusted — in the role of commerce raider. There should be some nice pickings coming. Prize Money — that great elusive — beckoned to him once again with the mockery of a will o' the wisp.

The men would also welcome the expected relaxation of the harshness of discipline necessary aboard a ship of the line. Small ships were notorious for their easier ways under competent commanders. Fox would have to think about that. He would tolerate no slackness whatsoever, none at all. There'd be floggings aplenty if the men thought otherwise.

The small detachment of ten marines aboard was commanded by their sergeant, there being a shortage of marine officers, and Fox made it his business to be pleasant to this man, a long-service worthy called Sergeant Cartwright. He was short and squat and heavily-built and rolled like a Dutch tub in a gale; but his men jumped when he spoke and yet did not seem to hate him, which made Fox wonder.

Truth to tell, Fox felt relief that there was no marine officer on board. For such a small vessel *Raccoon* was lucky to be allotted any marines at all, although they were considered essential aboard a King's ship to protect the officers from the lower deck. Had an officer come aboard, he would have been a sub-lieutenant, a runny-nosed sprig with no jaw, protruding eyes, a scraggy neck and a voice a fathom up his nostrils. Fox detested the breed.

He began to have ideas about *Raccoon.* He had no details of her capture, merely that she had been brought in and purchased into the Service; of course, had he had any details he would not have forgotten. So he did not as yet know what the British had done to her. There was no time now to go ashore again and find out; Mortlock would be inboard soon and they had to be ready to receive him in due style and then make sail and be clear of the coast before night. That was elementary. But, still and all, he thought she rode high in the water. He'd know better about her sailing qualities in detail once they were under way, and he looked forward to testing her in all kinds of weather; but he looked again in his mind's eye at that broad streak of copper he'd seen as he was rowed towards *Raccoon*. She could do with being lower in the water, and to hell with the estimated loss of speed through a deeper draught. If she'd been designed to a load line that was now above the water level, she'd act skittish, she'd roll too fast, she'd do all kinds of things any self-respecting brig would never do. And it wouldn't be her fault.

He had ideas on doing something about that, did George Abercrombie Fox, and they had no connection with ballast.

Within the couple of hours he was aboard before the captain stepped on to his quarterdeck, Fox had begun to impress his command on to the ship's company. He had all necessary items attended to, so that when Mortlock said: "Get underway at once, Mr. Fox," he could reply with confidence: "Aye, aye, sir," and give his own orders.

Gently, unremarkably, *Raccoon* headed out of Naples Bay with the Mediterranean before her.

Chapter Nine

Overside from *Raccoon* the xebec sloshed in the slight swell in a most dispirited fashion, her two lateen sails in an untidy heap across her deck, her square sails on the third mast shot away in an untidy raffle of cordage and ripped canvas. Her crew had been battened below and a marine with his scarlet coat with its white facings blazing in the sunshine stood guard over the hatchway. Fox could feel pleased. He stood looking over from the quarterdeck at *Raccoon's* second prize. The first, a fat brig, had been sent back with Master's mate Carker in command a week ago. For a time Fox feared that the Mediterranean had been swept clear of enemy shipping by the great and glorious victory of the First of August. But Bonaparte, now cut off in Egypt, needed supplies and if the low, fat trains of convoy shipping could not venture out of Toulon for fear of Nelson, small vessels could seek to make the passage. After all, hadn't Bonaparte himself crossed the Inland sea without sighting a single British sail?

So now he had taken a second prize. That old chimera prize money seemed to him to take on a more solid form.

They'd taken what they wanted from the prize, mainly fresh vegetables, and Fox, after sampling some of the wine, had ordered the rest stoved in. No sane man trusted British seamen near liquor in any conditions.

The problem he faced was a more subtle one. With Carker out of the brig, he should send Mr. Midshipman Johnny Prentiss away in command of the xebec. Lads of fourteen should be completely capable of handling a vessel like that, with a competent mate and a cheerful crew. He would only spare ten men, and a couple of marines. But Prentiss did not appear to Fox to be of the stuff from which future admirals are made.

The boy was not stupid, he was not particularly incompetent. He was all thumbs; but that was to be expected at such a time in a lad's life, along with the pimples. It was that he was so dull. Fox really didn't care if Johnny Prentiss sank or swam in the prize; but he did care, passionately, for the prize money she would bring him and his family.

"Now, Johnny," he heard Commander Mortlock saying to Prentiss as they stood together, looking at the xebec, "You'll find her a strange craft. Those lateen sails are beasts if you don't catch 'em just right —" Fox shut his ears to them. Of course, it was Mortlock's decision. Fox was greatly used to the feeling that everything aboard a vessel was his responsibility, and aboard *Raccoon* that was a fact. But in this, Mortlock had to take the responsibility and it had never occurred to that honourable young man that a fellow officer and gentleman could not manage a ship given the aid of a common sailorman or two.

Fox found Black Bill, the mate to whom the xebec would be entrusted. Black Bill, taciturn, be-whiskered, always chewing a cud, stood up from the raffle of rigging he was having spliced and set up as Fox jumped on to the xebec's deck.

Fox eyed him meanly.

"Mr. Prentiss is sailing her back, Black Bill. Are you man enough to handle that?"

"Aye, sir. I reckon this rig is handy enough."

Xebecs were among the fastest ships in the Mediterranean and Fox allowed himself feelings of pure joy the *Raccoon* had overhauled her without any undue strain. The brig was skittish, she needed ballasting down; but Fox could almost endure that continual worry for the sake of her fantastic turn of speed.

At Black Bill's deliberate turning of the intent of Fox's remark, Fox felt he had to press again. He might be doing more harm than good, however, he could not allow the prize to leave without doing all that he could to ensure her safe arrival. He could remember his own first command of a prize and that shouldn't happen to a dog.

Mind you, Prentiss was a gentleman, one of those to whom the Almighty had given the power of natural command and to whom ignorant seaman would listen and whom they would obey right up until death. For Fox, on the other hand, seamen like Black Bill had contempt and resentment.

Fox was used to that. He had a pair of fists and a pair of shoulders that could smash any man aboard.

He spoke more sharply than he intended. "Just see that he doesn't fall overboard or do anything else stupid. I'm relying on you to get him back. Understood?"

"Aye, aye, sir," and Black Bill went on with his splicing.

Fox returned to the brig, his back straight and his fists clenched. He had stepped out of line and been snubbed for his pains. To hell with the nobs and the guttersnipes all!

There had been an element of luck about the capture. Fox had himself laid and fired a nine pounder bowchaser and knocked away the xebec's square-rigged mast. He could allow himself the luxury of believing his gunnery had won the prize, and if he tired of that, of the luxury of believing that *Raccoon's* speed had won the chase. But no brig ought to be able to catch an xebec, surely? All Fox knew was that he felt more alive than he had done for many a long day. This life of roving and prize-taking suited him right down to the waterline.

That life had to end, and soon, for their orders instructed them to return to Naples at the end of a six weeks cruise, every ship and every man would be required for the offensive against the French.

The Russians and the Turks had combined together, although two more unlikely allies it was hard to conceive of, and sailing from the Dardanelles had attacked the French in the Ionian Islands. Malta was in process of being besieged by a joint British and Portuguese squadron. Bonaparte had toppled the long regime of the Knights of the Order of Saint John of Jerusalem and now the Directory sought to impose its Republican ideology upon the island. Lieutenant-General Charles Stuart with a small British army had taken Minorca in a dazzling and rapid campaign. His second in command, Thomas Graham of Balgowan, a man of impressive gifts and tremendous hatred of the French who had insulted his wife's body as it lay in her coffin, had taken up soldiering at the age of forty-five and was to do great things, or so considered Fox. Things were on the boil all over the Mediterranean.

And Nelson urged King Ferdinand to send his troops against the French. An Austrian, General Mack, would lead the Neapolitan Army against the French in Rome. Everywhere was bustle when *Raccoon* arrived in Naples.

They took aboard their prize crews, and Fox felt himself undergoing a strange kind of alien feeling of relief when he saw Mr. Midshipman Prentiss and Black Bill and the prize crew come aboard. He told himself that he was pleased they hadn't drowned; but he also thought more lovingly of the prize money to come.

The Neapolitan Army, to the strains of martial music and with flowers in their muskets and shakos, with their laughing-eyed *signorinas* dancing beside them, marched out. A British force sailed north and took Leghorn. *Raccoon* was kept busy. Another midshipman, Lionel Grey, was posted to them and the little brig creamed happily through the blue waters of the Mediterranean.

As soon as the veteran French army fired at the Neapolitans, the Italian officers dropped everything and ran away. The troops followed. The incompetent Mack turned himself over to the French for repatriation. Absolute horror and panic struck Naples. The dreaded French were once more on the march. The city would fall. All the terror of the French Revolution would burst about the nobles and lords and ladies of the ancient city.

The Kingdom of the Two Sicilies might lose Naples and its Italian possessions; but there was still Sicily, and to Sicily, therefore, the court and the nobles and the British colony would go. Only the British Fleet could save them. And only Nelson could deal with the emergency.

With their valuables to the value of millions — at least two million five hundred thousand pounds — packed away in casks labelled "Stores for the British Ships" they went aboard *Vanguard.* Nelson personally superintended the operation. Naples was in an uproar. Fox saw that the *lazzaroni,* the fractious, tough, devilish poor people of the slums would fight; but he did not give even them much of a chance against the trained veterans of the French army.

Commander Mortlock came aboard with orders.

George Abercrombie Fox knew how those orders would begin: "You are hereby required and directed to ...

To what?

Fox stared hungrily at Mortlock as the Commander went below to his cabin. They had remained in a state of armed neutrality. Mortlock let him get on with running the vessel. When orders which Fox could know only through Mortlock were necessary, as in the present circumstances they would speak frigidly and politely to each other. Mortlock had by now become only too well aware that the brig functioned by Fox's express will. Alone, or with his Master, Macbridge, who had returned aboard with a limp and no explanations for getting drunk on Nelson's birthday, Mortlock would be all at sea — and that made Fox feel a slight smile might be in order. Macbridge was the surly sort of Scot for whom Fox, remembering Thomas Graham of Balkowan, had only scorn. Fox kept him in his place with a rule of iron for there could with him be nothing even of the tentative hints of comradeship that had existed between Fox and Mr. Showell, the master of *Duchess.*

Mortlock, as would be inevitable in the circumstances, liked to savour his position and his moments of superior knowledge. He summoned Fox to the cabin and then hummed and hawed. Once he had told Fox their orders the old regime would resume. Fox waited in patience.

"Harrumph," said Mortlock, looking up from where he sat behind his desk. The cabin was small as it must be aboard a brig; but it was considerably larger than the cubbyhole that Fox inhabited when not on deck. Ninety men aboard, not a large crew for a vessel of *Raccoon's* size in naval terms, although monstrous for a commercial brig, had reasonable accommodations and Fox was as satisfied as he ever would be about naval conditions.

But when Mortlock told him their orders, Fox at once experienced a jolt of dismay.

"We're ordered to proceed to the Ponza Islands to take off subjects of King George before the dammed French get there." Mortlock tried to make himself sound official by using "proceed" instead of "sail". "A Lord Kintlesham and members of his family and suite."

Fox had never heard of any Lord Kintlesham — and did not particularly want to, either — but this honourable before him, this sprig of the nobility, surely ought to have done. Mortlock's lips were compressed. His face expressed distaste. Fox made one of his intuitive guesses and then realised that he wasn't being so clever; the truth was revealed plainly on the lumpy face of his commander.

"Yes, sir." he said, contenting himself with not giving an opening to Mortlock to empty out the spite in him. "I'll get under way at once, sir."

Mortlock's look of suppressed venom changed to one of surprise. He lifted his eyebrows.

"The charts are — surely, Mr Fox, you don't know where these dratted islands are, do you?"

Every officer should familiarise himself with the charts of waters where he expected to sail. Fox wanted to say: "You'd have benefitted by a commission under Captain Sir Cuthbert Rowlands." Instead, he said stiffly: "Yes, sir."

Although no love was lost between these two, Mortlock could not bring himself to challenge his first lieutenant's statement. But to him, Fox saw, it was clearly a mystery that anyone should know anything about remote and forgotten islands in the Mediterranean. He nodded, making it brusque.

"Very well, Mr Fox. I'll trouble you to get the vessel under way."

He should have said, Fox reflected, going up on deck and setting about it: "If you'll kindly get the vessel under way." But sprigs of the nobility were contemptuous of civilities they had no need to use.

Raccoon weighed and set sail and departed once more from the Bay of Naples. This time Fox set her head southwest, wishing to give Ischia a wide berth to leeward and not caring to run through the passage between that island and the mainland. Fox would always take the long way if the short way hazarded the ship — unless circumstances made no other alternative possible.

The panic-stricken city dropped away astern and then the volcanic cones of Vesuvius which smoked and smouldered and which since 1779 and its devastating eruption was surely going to blow up again soon. Wars and troubles brought volcanic eruptions, said the superstitious people. Standing on deck and unwilling for a moment to go below, for who would voluntarily miss seeing the splendours of the most beautiful bay in the world? Fox felt his thoughts drift back to his lost possessions still aboard *Duchess.* If they hadn't been tossed ashore by this time to rot in some Navy warehouse. Apart from his looted Spanish sword and the *main gauche,* he missed his books. He had the 1790 edition of Mr. Clerk of Eldin's book on naval strategy and tactics and he would have liked to have acquired the new 1797 edition. He had seen Mr. Clerk's theories triumphantly proved right up to the hilt at the Battle of the Nile. Perhaps more even than that he missed his Moliere. Of course, being in the middle of a long and bitter war against the French meant he had to keep quiet about his love of Moliere, especially given the chauvinistic pompousness of his naval contemporaries. He shared their patriotic feelings, without doubt; but also he could see no sense in denigrating a great playwright.

He looked up with a strict and intolerant eye to make sure all canvas was drawing, taut and firm, without a crease. *Raccoon* could be brought around soon to lie with the wind on her larboard quarter and so make a northing. There had been no time or opportunity to do anything about re-ballasting her, and she sailed heeled well over. He made up his mind, he would not set his royals until they had the wind more astern, and, with a nod to Carker who had the deck, went below. Fox would take the first watch at eight bells and he had items to plan and charts to study.

Of course he'd known where the Ponza Islands were — just off the Gulf of Gaeta only a short distance north west of Naples; but he had an idea that there were a number of them with weird outlandish names and he wanted to be in the full possession of all those names, and details, before he went to Mortlock to find out just which island it was they were bound for.

Assuming, of course, that the nincompoop knew.

Mortlock didn't know.

"Ponza Island, Mr Fox," he said, his lumpy features convulsed with the effort of thought. "You say the largest is called Ponza?"

"Yes, sir."

"Well, we'll go there, then. There doesn't seem any problem to me."

"Aye, aye, sir," said Fox, and rolled off.

He worked out their passage time and, because he felt reluctant to approach a strange landfall during the hours of darkness, took off some canvas. This had the immediate effect also of making *Raccoon* ride more comfortably. They should make landfall soon after dawn.

The islands were volcanic, low-lying, none above seventy feet or so, and they had, Fox noted with some grim amusement, been extensively used as a prison island in the past.

Just as the sun burst up over the horizon, he was called and went up on deck to see the dark flat wedges of land lying on the water. With a leadsman in the chains, he edged *Raccoon* in. The whole place looked deserted. Fox had one of his twinges. Danger for him lurked in these islands, he could sense it clearly in his left eye.

Chapter Ten

George Abercrombie Fox could trust no one aboard to pilot *Raccoon* around the islands. Even the Master, Macbridge, for whom Fox had a scorn he had constantly to moderate, could not be trusted. As the brig picked her way from island to island, from islet to islet, Fox could sink himself into the search and forget the sharp regrets he'd experienced on meeting Macbridge. Masters of King's Ships were almost invariably Masters, masters of their trade and masters of themselves.

They'd bypassed the most southerly island, Ventotene, and now that searches revealed Ponza itself to be empty of British citizens, they moved on to Palmarola and to Zannone. The dark volcanic rock jutted against the sea. The weather had been rough ever since they'd left Naples and now Fox saw clearly they were in for a blow. The sky held that aloof, metallic tint that betokened no good for mariners. Lee shores would be death very soon.

"We'll try Mentatone and then Zamba," Fox decided. "I don't want to be caught huddled in between these islands when the blow comes, so, if they are not there, we will have to make an offing." He stared up at Mortlock as that lumpy giant stood on his quarterdeck, king of all he surveyed. "We can return when the gale blows itself out, after all, the French can't land troops here if we can't keep station."

Mortlock nodded. Clearly, his bearing implied, he had other much more important considerations to worry about than the mere handling of the vessel.

For Fox the mission became a race between finding Lord Kintlesham's party on one of these god-forsaken islets and the onset of the gale. He ordered a gun to be discharged at fifteen minutes intervals, half the period of the sand glass on the quarterdeck. The gunner's mate, Joachim, a German who had been impressed off a Hamburg ship and had stayed on in the British service when faced with alternatives at home he did not wish to face, appeared to Fox steady enough, and he left the man to see to it. Joachim had a flaxen set of whiskers and a wide raffish smile and in general, for a petty officer, he was regarded by far the most favourably by the men.

Midshipman Lionel Grey had the watch when, after the echoes of the four pounder died away, a musket shot cracked out from a low islet off their starboard bow. Grey showed to Fox a glimmer of prospect, he was a year or so older than Prentiss and the two snotties did not see eye to eye. Fox maintained a strict neutrality between them and had to force himself not to be too strict on Grey out of a sheer stubbornness in recognising Grey as the better lad of the two. Now he said firmly: "Kindly put us a cables' length off that island, Mr. Grey. And have the cutter hoisted out and a boat's crew standing by."

"Aye, aye, sir," said Grey, eagerly, pleased at having something to do apart from normal watch-keeping routine. He was a strongly-built boy, fair-haired and lithe, with something in his looks of the Athenian, possibly accounted for by the straight-line angles of nose and forehead. His family would be of that great stratum of seafaring sons' parents, country doctors or parsons, most likely.

Another musket shot slapped echoes from the low volcanic slopes.

Mortlock came on deck with his telescope and trained it on shore. Fox hadn't bothered to do that. He'd seen no puff of smoke and therefore the firer or firers was or were not in view. *Raccoon* slid through the water. Deliberately, Fox went below. It was up to Grey and Mortlock now. He bent over the charts and his lower lip caught between his teeth.

When he heard Grey's half-broken voice shout: "Back your maintops'l!" and felt the way come off the brig, he went back on deck again.

Mortlock was, very officiously, giving orders about dropping anchor. Already men were moving out on their various errands — to the cathead, to the hawse-hole, standing by the cutter — and Fox, cursing himself for his own lack of foresight, had to do some quick thinking. Then he felt the old weariness sweep over him. Why should he worry? Let the fool get on with it. But, unbidden but unsleeping, the memories of his family rose. Of his mother, careworn, yet defiant against adversity still, of his small sisters, of his brothers trying to make a decent home when the father was dead and the eldest son was dead, when their main strength and sustenance came from George Abercrombie himself. To let himself down now was to destroy them. He would destroy anyone to save them.

He was blunt about it, within service discipline.

"A blow is coming on, sir, and I'd like to get the people ashore aboard as fast as possible and make an offing. If we have the anchor down —" He nodded towards those volcanic rocks. They could rip the bottom out of *Raccoon* and not even notice.

Mortlock's face knotted up again, a sign of his attempts at thought. Then he said: "Very well, Mr Fox. I shall prepare to receive the passengers aboard."

Fox took that as a direct invitation not only to belay the commander's last order, and to do as he wished, but to go ashore himself. He rapped his orders in a vicious and cutting way, told Grey to keep the vessel on station, told Mr Lassiter, the boatswain, to get the cutter in the water bloody quick, and then, when the boat's crew were seated at their oars and the cox'n was looking up, his hand on the line, waiting, Fox shinned down and took his place in the sternsheets.

"Give way," he said, and, for once disdaining to take the tiller, told the coxswain to steer for the cleft in the rocks from which he could now see excited figures waving at him.

A kind of crude jetty had been built of rough pumice blocks and there was depth of water to float a line-of-battleship. The cutter rounded to smartly and nudged against the rock, and Fox was off the boat and ashore before she had time to rise and sink to the tiny waves.

He stared at the group awaiting him with no real interest in them as persons but with a sinking feeling at to their numbers. Family — and suite?

My God — there were hundreds of them.

The man standing somewhat loosely before him was long and thin and dressed in an incredible old brown coat and a waistcoat that clearly did not fit. His breeches and stockings were torn and his shoes mere herring boxes. He carried a gold-knobbed cane and on his head which was covered with a white wig whose style and name were completely lost on Fox, he wore an old tricorne of a style not seen in years.

Yet his sun-and-wind-bronzed face was cheerful and his faded eyes peered with a glance at once distant and merry from a network of lines. He looked like a squirrel hunched over a nut in some leafy forest of Old England. He bowed.

Fox, not to be outdone, bowed in reply.

"Lord Kintlesham?" he said in his pricey voice.

"Who? Oh — ah — yes, of course. I keep forgetting." The noble peer looked out at *Raccoon*.

"Where are the rest of the ships? I believe there is water enough, I am told, to bring the largest transport in to the jetty. You need not bring the ferry boat into it at all."

Fox gasped. "Ferry boat?"

"Yes, yes, sir! That little boat out there — clear it away and bring in the ships for my beautiful marbles."

Had Fox been a noble lord himself he would no doubt have challenged this old maniac to a duel, so incensed was he at the insufferable ineptitude of calling his beloved *Raccoon* a ferry boat. He kept that polite and so-long and painfully cultivated smile on his face.

"His Majesty's Brig of War, *Raccoon,* has been sent to bring you and your family off, sir." He resolutely refused even to think about the suite, Although, now he looked, the hundreds his first appalled vision had seen had dwindled to about fifty, and they were clearly not English. The bright scarves around their heads, the gold rings in their ears — both ears, unlike an English sailorman who'd have a ring in one ear — their raffish loose clothing, told him they were Italians from the mainland. They'd have their own boats, then.

"Yes, yes," Lord Kintlesham was saying with a vague impatience. "Dear Sir William promised he would speak to Nelson, he wrote me by the last vessel to bring me supplies — that was too small to take my discoveries and so I sent it away." He looked again and this time with a fresh look as what Fox had told him struggled to penetrate. "Your little ferry — aha — boat, is all there is? No ships?" He swung around, suddenly animated, his face glowing with wrath that sat ill on that cheerful knotty countenance. "Sophie! Sophie! You'll have to leave your chests and luggage and folderols there won't be room."

A shrill female squawk penetrated the sultry air like a thirty-two pound shot splintering its way through a quarter gallery window.

"I will not leave a single thing, papa! Not one dress, not one fan, not one item of jewellery! They are all I have — would you desire me to walk about naked!"

A girl walked down towards the group by the jetty evidently coming from a tented camp higher up. Fox looked at her and his face drew up into a Turk's head knot of suffering. He daren't laugh. He turned away rapidly and said to Lord Kintlesham: "May I press your lordship to gather what belongings you wish to bring with you and then descend into the cutter as soon as maybe? We are due for the devil — I beg your pardon, my lord — for a big blow."

"But," protested the noble lord, puzzled, hurt, vague. "I can't possibly leave all my work here."

Desperately, Fox blundered on: "We can discuss the details aboard the brig, sir. Evidently there has been some misunderstanding. I am sure Admiral Nelson would have sent a larger ship had Sir William requested it, short though we are of vessels at the moment. But, I beg you, my lord, please come aboard my vessel now."

With a vague gesture as though it was all too much for him, Lord Kintlesham turned to his daughter. "Sophie — what your poor mother would say I do not know. We've to leave everything and go aboard that little boat." At her immediate protest he said: "I know it's hard, my dear, after all we've done here. But the French will not leave us in peace —"

"The French!" cried Sophie Kintlesham fiercely. "I hate them! Even if their dresses are nice, I hate them!"

Now Fox could look at her.

She was fat. He could not admit that she was plump, or well-formed, or Junoesque — she was fat. Her round cheerful simple face with two bright blue eyes and a frizzled hair piece of a corn colour looked exactly like that of a wax doll his sister Alice had played with until it had been left too near the fire and had melted to a state no art could resuscitate. Her white dress wrapped her like a tent of the Fencibles, and was rigged in as unhandy a fashion. Her feet were small and her calves bulged as she kicked fretfully at her skirts when she walked. Her thick upper arms were reddish brown and freckled. Fox, fearing the worst, looked at her moist upper lip; but she had no trace of a moustache. Her mouth was very red, and really rather nicely shaped, eminently kissable, but her cheeks were a coarse healthy red that would never do for candlelit drawing rooms.

He had at first thought her to be thirty or forty; but now he suspected she was still not yet twenty-one. She looked at him with a polite little smile and, Fox saw, she was nervous. She didn't know how to handle herself before even as unprepossessing an example of naval officer as Fox. The thought, treacherously, gave him no feeling of triumph; rather he felt sorry for her.

George Abercrombie Fox, feeling sorry for an aristocrat's daughter; that was a laugh of Jovian proportions.

"But my dresses —" she said, her voice broken. Then, her feelings breaking out again, and she said: "I hope you sink a dozen French ships, sir, a round dozen!"

"I hope so, too, milady," said Fox, and he found he was actually smiling at her. This would never do.

"I must press you to come aboard, my lord. We could leave you here, of course — you seem safe enough — and return when the gale blows out. That might be the wisest course."

Sophie took a hand. "No, papa. I don't trust the French. Damme, I don't want to lose all I have to some moustached French dragoon!"

Her father looked shocked in his old-fashioned way.

Fox stifled a chuckle. This fat little lady could quite easily be the driving force of the family. Were there more?

"How many are in your party, my lord?"

"Eh? Party? Oh — just Sophie and me."

Fox was shepherding them to the jetty now; but he relented. There would just be time. The air was even more sultry than ever and the wind furnace hot; when that wind died they'd be for it. "Pack what you need, please. I can give you ten minutes. No more."

Within the ten minutes, Lord Kintlesham and Sophie were in the cutter and the crew gave way with a will. Everyone knew what the weather portended. Fox scoured the horizon which remained brassy. No clouds yet. If that wind died before they cleared those islands they'd catch it.

Mortlock was anxious and angry and yet constrained to be polite to his guests. He eyed Sophie with a reserve that set icicles along Fox's spine, bowed with distant politeness to Lord Kintlesham, and, turning, was about to give orders to Fox until he realised that Fox had already shot the hands aloft and got *Raccoon* under way.

They pulled free and Fox, watching those cruel volcanic rocks drop away, felt a profound thankfulness. He ordered the royals to be set and that made *Raccoon* leap about. Mortlock queried the order, and, about to order them off again, was prevented by Fox's quiet words.

"We must get as far as we can, sir. I promise you I'll have all the canvas off her long before the gale hits."

If he didn't, of course, there would be little chance of a court-martial; *Raccoon* and her crew would not survive.

He set lookouts to scan every inch of the horizon. As long as the furnace breeze held they could run out to sea. But, all too soon, that wind died. The sails flapped and the quartermaster reported he was unable to hold the course.

"Take the canvas off her, Mr. Grey," said Fox.

In a dead, flat calm, Fox ordered a storm jib to be run up. He made all the preparations for riding out a gale that were needful. The guns were triple-lashed and dogged. The yards were given extra lashings. Every chink on deck was plugged. He had life-lines strung along the deck. The wheel was fixed with relieving tackle, and the lines were looped and ready to keep the quartermaster and the men at the relieving tackle from being swept overboard.

And all this in a dead, flat calm.

Fox turned as Lord Kintlesham said in his ear: "I confess I do not understand — ah — ships and things of the sea. But your preparations seem strange —"

"I think it would be best if you went below, my lord. Your daughter as well."

For Sophie was standing by the quarterdeck rail, lifting her head so that brazen light fell across her corn-coloured hair and haloed it with a golden aureole, her whole fat figure indicative of high romantic allusions.

Fox sighed.

He thought he knew the breed. Fat her body might be; but her head would be stuffed with knightly romances, courtly fairy-tales, her system surfeited with emotions and unfulfilled longings, her virginity an affront and a treasure to her.

"Deck there!" yelled the foretop lookout. "Clouds off the starboard bow!"

By the time Fox jumped up to look out the clouds had risen above his horizon from the deck. Black and ominous, swirling, flickering with lightning, they rushed down on *Raccoon.* "Get down on deck!" he yelled to the lookout. "Brace yourselves!" To Kintlesham and Sophie he was brisk. "Get below!" He dashed back to the bight of rope by the taffrail. Everything was ready. Here it came. Blackness, swirling darkness, the enormous noise of wind — the gale struck.

Chapter Eleven

The storm that now enveloped *Raccoon* was one that
Nelson himself described as the worst he had ever experienced.
Whether or not he said that merely to lend the thrill of extremes
to Sir William's wife, to admit her to a supreme moment of his
life and out of the natural desire to please her own fervent
imaginings, is of no importance. During that storm the
youngest prince of the Neapolitan royal family, a boy only six
years old, died aboard Vanguard, cared for until the end and
wrapped in Lady Hamilton's arms. She never boasted of her
devotion. When Fox heard about it he recognised a strong
fibrous resilience in her character he had seen in Kitty Higgins.

That storm wrenched the guts out of a man. It flung
people about and smashed ribs, it filled the tween-decks with
vomit, it ripped spars from ships and stove in stout planking,
Raccoon lived for two reasons, and perhaps the more important
of those two was the latter. She was a fine, seaworthy vessel,
and George Abercrombie Fox conned her all during the height
of the gale.

The carpenter made his rounds, sounding the well,
testing the fabric. The boatswain kept a wary eye on her spars.

The gunner's mate checked the lashings of the guns. The sailmaker down in his forward flat methodically prepared a fresh storm jib in case of need. Everyone not needed on deck was battened below. Fox, lashed to his position by the taffrail, kept one eye aft for the roaring avalanches of cream and green marbled water hounding them and threatening every instant to poop them, and one eye forward to the whole tilting mass of *Raccoon.* How he did this he could never explain; it was a gift given to sailormen beloved by the gods.

He could shout his commands to the men at the wheel and the distance was such that they could hear through the uproar of the wind. Later he shifted his position as the gale mounted and the shriek of the wind drowned even the loudest shout. The noise boomed and battered inside his head. They were going up and down a crazy distance as the waves rolled past. Under bare poles and with the scrap of canvas set on their jib stay they kept their stern to the wind and sea and scorched out into the Mediterranean.

When it was all over and the blue sky and the sunshine returned, like furtive strangers, Fox felt both exhausted and exhilarated.

With grim intolerance, he set the men to cleaning up the vessel and, under topsails with the headsails and the driver, they clawed back for the island of Zamba.

This time Fox took *Raccoon* in alongside the jetty. He had seen to it that there were more than enough coir fenders out. That sharp pumice could lacerate his vessel's side and he wasn't having anything like that done to *Raccoon,* not after the gallant way she had brought them through the gale. The Italian workmen clustered. Fox jumped down on to the jetty and, followed by Lord Kintlesham and a body of men, he strode inland.

"Sir William, you see is a great antiquary, and he and I have found much that will startle the pundits of London and

Europe." Lord Kintlesham had revealed his abiding passion. If he could dig up an old marble face with a nose and an ear missing and give it some outlandish Greek or Roman name, he was happier than a man flying his own flag and listening to his first eleven gun salute.

Followed by the gesticulating crowd of Italians and the British seamen glad to have the opportunity to stretch their legs on land, Fox passed the small tented camp and soon came to the site. Here massive blocks of marble and limestone lay tumbled in inextricable confusion. To one side a cleared space had been piled with straw-packed bundles. Sunshine warmed the scene.

Lord Kintlesham beamed with the pride of a father seeing his first-born.

"Ponza was called Pontiae in ancient times, Mr Fox. It was a kind of New South Wales to the Romans." He chuckled at the conceit. "They banished prisoners here. Caligula s sisters were here, and Nero, Germanicus's eldest son." He waved vaguely about the horizon. "As for Pandateria, well, Octavia, Nero's divorced wife, was sent there. And Julia and her daughters Agrippina. I suppose they were lucky not to have been killed." He patted a piece of marble, looking like mouldy cheese, protruding from the straw packing.

Fox looked silently at the great mass of marble. One of those blocks, he estimated, must weigh four tons. And Lord Kintlesham had been busy. He just didn't bother to count. *Raccoon* could not possibly take them. A thirty-two pounder and truck weighed three tons. And whoever heard of a brig armed with thirty-two pounder guns?

Mind you, Fox drifted easily into his own private day dream, mind you, if he had his way he'd re-arm a brig or a sloop and then the French would feel the old iron fist even more solidly slogging behind their ear — he came out of that pleasant imagining to hear Sophie panting up to the party.

"Mr. Fox, you will take my father's marbles? Please? We have worked so hard here —" She smiled at him, her fat face coy and sticky as candy left before an oven.

"I'm afraid, milady, that *Raccoon* would not swim with the weight you have collected here."

She pouted. "But you could take something off, couldn't you?"

Fox shut his eyes. When he opened them he was as urbane as ever with a lady. But she was staring into his face, and her bright blue eyes clouded, her soft lips trembled. She must, thought Fox, remembering, love her father dearly.

"We could take some, of course," he said, cautiously.

As he had expected and dreaded, the Kintleshams took that as complete co-operation on his part. The crude sleds with which the Italian workmen transported the stones were slid out, much heaving and straining rolled the first marble into place, it was lashed down, and then the procession hauled it to the jetty.

Fox cocked an eye up to the main yardarm. Any attempt to whip this lot up would crack the yard like a toothpick. He called for Mr Lassiter and supervised the setting up of a pair of sheer-legs. As they did not have a launch they could not use her masts; but Fox decided to use the spare topmasts housed amidships. The men worked with will. Anything novel, anything with a challenge to it, could inflame them. Fox was sure enough of Lassiter to let him get on with constructing the pair of sheers, using canvas and the regulation eleven round turns and ten riding turns. The tackles would have to be nicely calculated. The purchase was shackled to the strops placed around the head lashing. The tackles to secure the heels of the sheer legs and the span tackle between them — if they opened suddenly with a marble bust of Aphrodite swinging from the purchase the deck of *Raccoon* would be punctured and not by love — he made very sure were firmly set up. The Navy was accustomed to shifting heavy weights with man power and

114

block and tackle. With the guy pendants and guy purchases with their necessary thimbles and blocks all running sweetly — Fox noted with grim approval that Lassiter made sure of that before reporting to his first lieutenant — the pair of sheer legs was ready to swing the first bust aboard.

Fox had elected to use tarred cordage, he always preferred the little extra degree of security that afforded, hawser-laid, and when the topping lift brought the sheer legs up into position the sling could be attached to the first load. The centre of gravity was kept as low as possible. Men tailed on to the purchase fall and, at the boatswain's signal, given at a nod from Fox, they walked away handsomely. The marble lady — whoever she was — rose into the morning Italian sunshine.

Fox discovered that Sophie had a strange predilection for following him about.

She chattered on about dear Sir William, and how her papa was also a member of the Royal Society and a fellow of the Society of Antiquaries and of the Dilettanti, and of how he had discovered this pagan Roman temple on Zamba, although, she confided this with a great show of shy diffidence, she herself considered it quite probable that the temple was of a much earlier date, possibly Greek or even one of the mysterious Etruscan erections. She had followed her father on his antiquarian expeditions for as long as she could remember, her mother had died during one of them, and she, it was clear, conceived of no other life. Fox had not been surprised to find an English nobleman and his daughter in such a strange situation, the craze for antiquities went hand in hand with the eccentric character of the English nobility. They were all over the continent digging and sketching and measuring, and even this war with France had barely curtailed their eager activities.

Fox supposed it would be nice to do that kind of thing if you had the money to waste.

"And Papa has written a great deal on the problems of accurate dating for the Philosophical Transactions of the Royal Society." She looked fat and ungainly and sweaty and yet she hopped about agilely enough, following Fox as he superintended the loading.

The Italians were working with a will that Fox would have found puzzling had he not been aware that they were concerned over the appearance of the French. It had been a wise thing for the Kintleshams to go aboard *Raccoon;* a French ship of vague description had been seen off the islands. No doubt the storm would have driven her away; but she would be back.

Lord Kintlesham had expressed himself with some vigour on the subject of Bonaparte's expedition to Egypt. "Think of all the wonderful discoveries to be made there! And to think, as we must, that they will be carried back to France instead of England! It makes me boil."

Nothing much else, Fox surmised, would make the old peer excited. And Sophie was devoted to him. Yet she kept on following Fox about, and had mentioned more than once her admiration for his handling of the brig during the gale. To Fox that had been routine, yes, the storm had been a bad one, but the honourable Sophie Kintlesham mustn't think that riding out a storm made a naval officer a naval hero.

She took every opportunity to cling on to his arm as they negotiated the rocks.

Fox tried to slip her hawse on to Commander Mortlock; but Sophie would have nothing of the honourable commander.

With a naive frankness he found touching — and then rounded on himself with bitter scorn for applying that kind of thinking to an honourable, a sprig of the nobility — she said that Mortlock was not a very nice man. His father and her papa had been involved in a terrible argument the details of which were too horrible to go into, and she was only sorry that such a fine officer as Mr Fox had to serve under such a rake and rapscallion. Fox felt he ought not to listen, and then with his own brand of cynical disregard of rules and etiquette knew he didn't give a damn for the fine scruples of these people. If this funny fat little girl wanted to get it off her chest, then let her.

He drove the men on. Lord knew what was happening back at Naples. Orders were to go direct to Palermo. He wanted to get back there, unload all these stones, and then get out to sea and take a few rich prizes. The family in Rotherhithe needed all the money he could send them. Every penny. They took all his pay and prize money, the agents paying it direct. Fox subsisted on what he could make or steal at sea.

The man he had posted as a lookout on the highest rocky outcrop of the little island was relieved at regular intervals. Looking over the Mediterranean, even when the air carried a hint of a severe winter to come, was tiring to the eyes. He didn't want fatigue to blot out the topsails of a French frigate or corvette. They'd be caught here like rats in a trap.

As soon as he started thinking of French ships he felt the old resentment rising in him. The British never seemed capable of building ships to equal the French or Spanish examples. He'd been around shipyards all his early life, watching his father labouring for practically nothing, urging on his elder brother John in his ambition to become a carpenter and thus support the family, and the shock of finding such superiority in enemy vessels had still not completely passed away. Blackwall had never been able to turn out a brig as fast and efficient as *Raccoon,* for example.

The Times had once even had the nerve to applaud the French decision to build a whole new fleet of liners and frigates, claiming that it would not be long before they were all captured and in use by the Royal Navy. A fine way to plan the construction for a country's first line of defence! Mortlock, of course, took no part in the loading of the brig for this was properly the duty of the first lieutenant. Fox watched critically as the copper sheathing sank below the waterline. His theories would have a try out now, for sure. Steadily the men worked on. They sweated and heaved, tailing on to the falls, hoisting the massive blocks of stone. Fox reflected that the decision had been his but Mortlock had tacitly consented, for his orders called on him to transfer Kintlesham and his effects. Fox doubted if anyone, apart from Sir William, had known that those effects consisted of many tons of marble.

Ineffectual though Mortlock was, he remained the captain.

With much care and a great deal of packing — and much cursing — the marbles were stowed in the hole. The monuments of another age were on the first stage of the journey that would end in some high-arched gallery of England. Fox wondered; but his orders were clear enough.

Sophie was prattling on about a Spanish Don, whose tongue-twisting name she had off pat, Inigo Lopez de Mendoza, Marquis of Santillana, who had, it seemed, written what Sophie termed a kind of imitation Dante poem all about the sea battle of 1425 off Ponza. He'd called it the *Comedieta de Ponza.* Fox made no comment beyond a polite phrase or two. He did not consider the sea battles in which he had taken part comedies; although there had been some comedians involved, that was for sure.

All this remembrance of old times, this chatter from Sophie, the regular swinging aboard of Lord Kintleshams antique marble heads and torsos, the continual expectations of a sighting from the lookout, all were wearing on a man's nerves. He realised with something of an unpleasant shock that all these items in the catalogue were a normal part of his existence in one form or another, with the exception of Sophie. She was completely artless, naive, lacking in any attempts at drawing-room coquettishness, and yet here she was simpering on his arm, her fat face screwed up against the sunshine that grew hotter by the minute, making conversation with him, letting her bright blue eyes rove over his face and then shielding them with eyelids lowered in maidenly confusion.

Nothing in what he was doing should trouble him in the slightest. It was Sophie who was wearing on him.

His relief when the lookout sent down a ship's boy as a messenger was comical. He felt the constriction of Sophie's continual attentions slacken at the same time as he experienced a sharp pang of anxiety over *Raccoon*.

Four large boats were approaching the island. Fox made a decision in his habitual immediate style.

"That's the last torso," he said as an immense pair of breasts lacking arms, stomach or navel, swung up to hover menacingly over the brig's hatches. "Stow that away and then strike all this lumber." His voice rose. "Watch that straw packing, you bunch of idle layabouts! If you scratch my deck I'll have you holystoning for a month of Sundays!"

"Get the men all aboard, Mr. Prentiss, Mr. Grey, come with me and fetch your telescope."

With that Fox started off at a jog-trot across the track of the sleds, jumping scattered rocks, began to climb up to the outcrop. Black Bill had the watch. He nodded across to the far side of the island.

"Four of 'em, sir. Big. Dipping lugsails. French."

Grey flopped down beside him. Fox took the telescope and pulled the brass tubes out. Through the lenses he quickly centred the leading boat. He could see white water creaming away from the bows which raked up sharply and were painted in a zigzag pattern of bright colour. The boat was crowded with the blue uniforms of French foot.

He made no comment although fully aware that Mr. Midshipman Grey was all agog to know what he would do now. Black Bill rolled his head and spat a stream of tobacco juice into the pumice. Fox ignored that. He traversed the telescope, checked each of the boats. All were the same except the last, and that carried a small piece of artillery, probably a four pounder, with its wheels chocked up. They did not carry any naval artillery, and that was a relief. Probably they were local boats commandeered by the French. As to why they were coming here he just didn't give a damn at the moment. They were coming, and that was the datum he must consider.

He handed the telescope back to Grey.

"Tell me how many men you make it, Mr. Grey. Sailors and soldiers separately."

He rubbed his eyes. That old left eye would go blinking on him now, for sure.

A distant shout arrested his attention. A man darted out from the rocks below him and began to wave his arms and his shako at the boats. His shako! Now Fox could see his blue uniform. The boats were still some way off to the man, and they might not have seen him yet. But in the next few minutes they would. Part of the mystery was explained. During the storm a French ship or boat carrying soldiers had foundered. This man must be a survivor who had reached Zamba, no doubt his comrades had reached other islands and been rescued. But he would bring the boats unfailingly to Zamba — and he must have been watching the British activity.

Grey said: "I make it twenty seamen and about a hundred and twenty soldiers, sir." Then, lowering the telescope, he added: "There's one down there, sir!"

Black Bill spat. "He'll need to be sent to hell." He pushed forward the pistol he had been issued, which, together with his cutlass, was standard equipment for a landing party, of which Black Bill formed a part. He took aim.

"Belay that, you lubber," said Fox. He spoke evenly. "A pistol shot will bring them here faster than he will shouting."

"But, sir," said Grey. "He'll attract their attention in a moment. I'd better get down there and silence him."

The boats creamed along, the wind bellying their sails.

"No time, Mr. Grey."

Fox took out that carefully folded black silk kerchief. He looked around, found a piece of rock that ought to fly true. It was a long shot. He shook the kerchief out, triangled it, placed the stone in the centre, took it cunningly by the corners. Then he half rose just enough to give him swinging room but not so much he might not escape observation from the boat, if he was lucky.

Black Bill spat again. Grey gave a choked sound that Fox, concentrating, did not bother to try to recognise. He thought of Midshipman Lunt and that sentry on the Laronne, and then he became just an eye and an arm and an extension of the sling.

Cunning, sharpened by a hungry belly on the marshes of the Thames, impelled that sling. He let fly. The man below him flung up both his arms, dropped his shako, spun around and then sprawled face down on the rocks.

Fox crawled back off the skyline, stood up, dusted his breeches and began to stow his kerchief.

"Come along, now," he said.

Grey was beside him, looking at him with a most odd expression.

"My God, sir!" exclaimed Grey. "That was magnificent!"

Wasn't that what Lunt had said? These young snotties had no vocabulary.

Black Bill was hefting his cutlass, his barred eyebrows drawn down. "Begging your pardon, sir," he said, with an expression new to his relations with Fox. "That was a fair old shot, sir. I ain't seed anything like it afore."

121

"We're not out of this yet," said Fox, and then strode off in front of them, sliding and scampering down the slope. This pumice would ruin his shoes. The damned Navy wouldn't care. And he could scarcely claim they'd been lost in battle — not with a sling and a single soldier, he couldn't.

Mind you, he knew enough of the ways of corruption in the Service to steal what he had to.

At the jetty all the British were aboard the brig. Fox told the Italians that the French were on the way, and the response indicated clearly what would happen in that quarter. The Italians' boats were beached over on the other side of the island, and they could escape without being seen if they hurried and were lucky. Amid a great amount of gesticulation and invective, the Italians pushed off.

Fox regarded them with the genial and unthinking good-natured contempt with which almost all Englishmen regarded foreigners. If suddenly presented with a question about them, he'd probably have responded with: "Look out for their breaths," garlic being an exotic. As to the famed and feared knives and daggers of the continentals, any man who'd served aboard a British man-o'-war knew how to use a knife, and Fox had slit enough throats to know how to do the job properly and to protect his own.

A tearful Sophie met him as he came aboard.

"All that work, to be left behind, for the dratted Froggies, it makes me cross, Lud, it makes me cross!"

Fox had an absurd desire to comfort her; but the idea of patting her fat shoulder, which would probably shake like rotten leg of mutton, so astounded him with its ludicrous impossibility that he turned rapidly away and shouted a few oaths he guessed would be incomprehensible in their sea-flavour to Miss Sophie. She was a barrel of lard, with her waist line like a Spanish hundred and twelve! The men jumped to his commands. He went below to find Mortlock sitting at his desk drinking some inferior Madeira he'd picked up somewhere. Mortlock looked up, sullenly.

"Well, Mr. Fox?"

"Vessel all ready to get under way sir. Four boatloads of French soldiers — ordinary regiment of the line by the look of them — putting in to the island; but we have time to clear well before they reach this side."

"Froggies, you say, the devil take 'em!" Mortlock stood up, automatically bending his head beneath the beams. His eyes looked glassy. "I'd dearly love to fight 'em — but with all these stones aboard, why, man —" He gestured slovenly. "We're like a damned Thames lighter, filled with broken bricks and crewed by illiterate Thamesside bastards. Mark my words —" He glowered down on Fox who had remained as stiff as a Guardsman's ramrod at mention of Thames and Thamesside bastards — his father and mother were properly married and the parish register duly indicated that important fact — and Mortlock went on to blister the air about the Kintleshams. "Mark my words, Mr. Fox, they're a bad bunch. Don't get mixed up with 'em. Lord Kintlesham swindled my father, and then had the infernal cowardice to refuse to fight a duel like a gentleman. If it wasn't for the influence with Lady Hamilton —" Then he caught himself and turned owlishly on Fox. "Well, Mr. Fox? What are you waiting for? Get the ship underway at once — do I have to do everything?"

Fox breathed in when he reached the deck, snapped out his orders in a way that made the men jump quite as much as the colts in the hands of the mates. Still, he had learned a little more about the Kintleshams. A tragic recollection of his brother Archie and the comrades of their branch of the London Corresponding Society flashed into his mind. The British Sans-Culottes, they'd been called. Jacobins — Jacobins were prissy milk-and-water revolutionaires beside them.

Well, all that was in the past, dead and buried. Now he had a vessel of His Britannic Majesty King George the Third to take out to sea and navigate safely to Palermo. Life had its funny little ups and downs and in betweens.

The wind blew with a regular rate from the north east that pleased him. He felt in his bones that it would back to the northward fairly soon, and that would be even better provided the weather held. Under easy sail *Raccoon* headed away from Zamba.

Strange that he should think of Archie and the L.C.S. Here he was becoming embroiled with a nobleman and his fat daughter. She simpered like a sick cow. He had no time for aristocrats, for the clique that governed or their equally aristocratic opponents. The working man had had his chance and thrown it away. Now Fox devoted all his energy to staying alive and to providing for his family. The price of bread was still a scandal. After those awful winters when the prices reached heights quite out of the reach of the poor, following on bad harvest, he had taken a solemn vow never to let anything — *anything at all* — stand in the way of providing for his family. He was still that same George Abercrombie Fox. No fat girl whose father was a Lord could possibly change that.

They were rounding the point of pumice rock that marked the end of the island, and before them lay the open sea. He growled a curt order at the quartermaster and that man, one Hawkins, repeated it, with his eternal "Aye, aye, sir", *Raccoon* leaned to the breeze and hissed through the water.

Sheer rock faces passed away to windward, furrowed and fissured by weather. A few birds wheeled and called. The sun glinted from the sea as they lay over on the starboard tack. In a moment he could give the order to tack when they were well clear of the point. He liked plenty of sea room, did George Abercrombie Fox.

"Sail ho!" The man in the maintop was hallooning down. "Tg'nt sails, three on 'em! Just clearing the point!"

A ship, then.

"Can you make out what they are?" Fox bawled up.

"Don't reckernise 'em, sir. French. Sure o' that, sir."

Goddammit to hell! A French ship — a frigate if he was unlucky, a corvette if he was not quite so unlucky — standing right across his course, from windward, able to sweep out from the point and have him immediately under her guns.

He waited in an expectation that would have resulted in an explosion of frustrated anger in anyone not so accustomed to concealing his true emotions as Fox. He sent down for Mortlock. Not, Fox told himself with cynical realism, he'd be of any more use than anyone else. A bowsprit emerged from the point. The lookout yelled again. "Frigate, sir! Big 'un — forty-gunner."

"Put your helm up," Fox said quietly to the quartermaster. As *Raccoon* came around and the men scurried to the braces, Fox saw the big French frigate clear the point and come racing down on them, all sails pulling, and even as he watched, her port lids went up and her guns showed, grinning at him like a row of sharp black teeth.

Chapter Twelve

George Abercrombie Fox stared ahead at the lowering rock precipices of the island of Zamba towards which *Raccoon* was racing. The wind was almost directly aft now. The French frigate sailed with a billowing rush from the point and with the wind hurtling both craft on they headed for the rocks. Fox had lost all the sea room he had been aiming for. Between the shore ahead, which extended in its trend south-westward further out than the point to north east he had been clearing, and the pursuing frigate, he was between that devil and deep blue sea so well-known to sailormen.

Mortlock came on deck, doing up his uniform coat with one hand and wiping his lips with the other. His lumpy face showed that he had been trying to put his thoughts in order.

"Beat to quarters, Mr. Fox," he said thickly. "Clear the ship for action."

"Aye, aye, sir," said Fox. It was the only order anyone could give now that made some sense.

As the drums roared through *Raccoon* and all the preparations so familiar to Fox were made, with a lick of the smartness he had tried to drill into the crew in the seven or so weeks they'd been together, Fox walked aft and stared narrowly at that pursuing shape. She was a forty gunner, all right. From the cut of her jib and the way the water spurned back from her beak Fox could form an opinion of her class and possible armament. As always, thought of guns and technical matters allied to guns absorbed him.

She'd more than likely have a measurement of a thousand tons or thereabouts, and be armed with twenty-eight long twenty-four pounders on her main deck, with a dozen carronades, twenty-fours or possibly thirty-twos, on her quarterdeck and a couple of long eighteens or something similar on the forecastle. She would almost certainly have more guns than her legend; but those would be more than sufficient to blow *Raccoon* and her pop-gun four pounders out of the water.

Fox went back to the wheel. Mortlock was standing there like some renowned hero from myth, constantly half-drawing his sword and thrusting it back into its sheath. He studiously ignored Lord Kintlesham and Sophie who stood together on the opposite side of the quarterdeck, looking back at the French frigate.

"Lud," he heard Sophie exclaiming, her round chin lifted so that, for the moment, her one and half extras were ironed out into a taut line, "How I'd like to spit in that Froggie's eye!"

Fox approached. "I feel it would be best if you went below," he said politely. "Your lordship, I feel sure, would not wish me to have to take the responsibility of feeling guilty over the safety of your lordship's daughter."

"Tut, man!" said Lord Kintlesham. "We'll go below if we have to, but, damme, I ain't seen the feller fire a shot yet."

Fox looked at him, shocked. All the vagueness was gone. Sophie's thick features were contorted into a fierce rictus of hatred. Her big body thrust against the rail as she gripped with her two tiny fists. He'd noticed before how small her hands and feet were compared to the grossness of the rest of her. Her nose was small, too; small and not pug-like, which he would have expected.

"Just think, papa," said Sophie, and the tenor of her words, in the present desperate circumstances, shocked Fox even more. "If we're sunk, all the discoveries will sink to the bottom. Perhaps they won't be re-discovered for another two thousand years."

"If the Froggies sink my antiquities, I'll — I'll — Lord Kintlesham with his thin frame and lanky pose looked positively ludicrous, like a skeleton dancing enraged around a feast that his lack of a stomach precluded him from enjoying.

Jack Sprat and his wife, thought Fox, and went back to the wheel.

Now he had to do what he had to do — once before he'd done something similar with *Invulnerable* — he ignored Mortlock. He sent for Midshipman Grey who was in command of the starboard battery.

"Listen carefully, Mr. Grey. We are going to weather that point ahead —"

At Grey's calm nod, Fox felt anger, which he quelled instantly. Didn't the jackanapes know how dangerous what he proposed doing was? Here was Grey acting as though what Fox said and did were the most normal events he could imagine. The French frigate clearly expected the British Brig to go on to the starboard tack to round the point; then all the French captain would have to do would be to cut across the base of the subtended triangle and shoot them to pieces if they did not strike or watch them run aground if they so chose.

"At my word of command, Mr. Grey, I want you to have the men at the braces haul away *instantly*. We'll go on the larboard tack. When we tack back we must go through stays so fast it'll be like you leaping out of a bedroom window when the husband comes in the door." Grey was actually smiling. This was intolerable, clear insubordination. "We'll be scraping that rock. If there's the slightest delay we'll be in trouble. If we miss stays, if we go in irons — migod! — we'll go down on those rocks and be smashed to splinters."

Fox had to haul up there, all-standing. Despite his own most rigorous precepts, here he was attempting to instil in this youngster all the dangers of the situation and a grave understanding of those dangers, and he was maundering on like a washerwoman down by the Thames when the Fleet sailed in. He screwed his face into a blank expression. "Very good, Mr. Grey. Tell Mr. Lassiter to have his mates handy and ready with their starters."

"Aye, aye, sir."

Raccoon was sliding through the water now. Fox could clearly feel the difference in her motion caused by the tons of marble antiquities in her hold. She cut a deep furrow through the sea. Those marble relics were the finest pieces, especially selected by Lord Kintlesham when he realised he could not take all his discoveries. Somehow, Fox didn't give a damn for them in any ordinary sense, he didn't give a damn for the Frenchmen breathing down his neck, or for the noble lord and his suet-dumpling daughter; he did give a very big damn for his own skin.

The rocks were leaping towards them now. He could see the spray forced upwards as the wind-driven waves broke against their unyielding feet. The water would wear away that pumice rock; it would splinter his brig into kindling in an instant. Only one thing was in his favour; he had plenty of water beneath his keel.

Mortlock was frowning, fingering his sword, staring back. Now he stalked over to Fox.

"We're running away, Mr. Fox."

"Yes, sir."

He stalked back, and as he went he shot a look of pure hatred at the Kintleshams. Fox considered he should think himself lucky the Kintleshams were aboard. They were the only factor aboard causing this lumpy-faced idiot to stop throwing his ship and his men away in a foolhardy and suicidal attack on the French frigate.

She'd have three hundred men aboard — bound to.

Fox would attack if he was ordered to, and if he had to. But, in the present circumstances, no one was going even to reprimand him if he made off.

The rocks were nearer now. Aboard the frigate they'd have hands to braces ready to go about. They'd go on to the starboard tack. The frigate wouldn't be able to come around so swiftly as *Raccoon.* Now the white water was a continuous leaping line at the base of the cliffs.

Time.

"Go about, Mr. Grey!" bawled Fox. To the quartermaster, he shouted: "Helm hard over, quartermaster."

Raccoon heeled, she whipped around to larboard, surging in the water, leaning over. The canvas slatted once, and then tautened and she was heading back and into the island. Fox waited. The frigate was already turning away, in the opposite direction. Fox was heading straight for the island they had just left.

"And again, Mr. Grey! Lively, now!"

Raccoon heeled to larboard again, white water spurning, the wind hammering her canvas, whining in her rigging. She came up, hesitated, fell off, then as the rudder bit she straightened up, sailing full for the open sea. The frigate was on an almost parallel course ahead and to larboard, trying to come around again. Fox watched her grimly.

Raccoon had gone in a circle, in effect wearing around and passing the frigate astern. Now it all depended on speed.

He bawled fresh orders and men raced aloft to set the studding sails. Under every stitch of canvas that would draw *Raccoon* headed out to sea. The frigate was edging in. She was closing her side of the triangle. Only the most elementary of calculations told Fox that there would be a brief moment when the two sides of that triangle met. He looked down over the quarterdeck rail. The men were standing to their guns, looking across at the frigate.

"Larboard battery!" He didn't turn back to Mortlock. "Triple-shotted. Give it to 'em as we pass. Wait until every gun bears." Then, as was usual on such occasions, Mortlock having omitted the formality, he added one or two platitudinous words about the British sailor, and Monsieur Johnny Crapaud, and how for the honour of the flag and of *Raccoon* Englishmen always struck home to victory. He finished by saying: "and if any man jack of you doesn't do his duty I'll have the hide off his back!"

The wind in his hair, the sun on his face, the feel of the ship as she raced over the waves with every stitch of canvas taut and satisfyingly full, the lick of spindrift over the bows — this was life as he understood it. In a moment he would be facing the hellish destruction of a broadside, and everything might finish in blackness. His left eye began to exhibit that devilish ring of purple and black. He held himself very still, very straight. He concentrated on the subtended angles of the vessels. He gave low-voiced commands to the quartermaster at the wheel and *Raccoon,* squeezing past the point which was to windward and the frigate edging up from leeward, aimed for the gap.

They'd get through all right, his seamanship had seen to that. But they wouldn't escape without one broadside. He had to hold on, now. Nothing else mattered but getting *Raccoon* safely through that narrowing gap of clear water.

It would be close — closer than he liked.

Their pipsqueak four pounders would scarcely dent the scantlings of the frigate. But they had to go on now.

Mortlock was staring at the frigate, shaking his fist at her. Then it seemed to Fox as though the masts and yards of sails of the frigate swooped towards him. He was aware of the guns going off, of the four-pounders hacking their brittle puffs of smoke, and of the deeper boom of the twenty-four pounders in reply and the banks of smoke rolling. Haze obscured his vision. He saw a marine firing his musket from the waist suddenly reel back with blood spouting from what was left of his face. He heard a halliard snap. He felt the drum and rebound of the brig's deck as the guns smashed back on their trucks. He caught a glimpse though swathes of smoke of the frigate's side and her main chains with men leaning out firing muskets, then a single glimpse of her bowsprit with the fierce dark figures of men on her forecastle, and they were past and drawing away.

He bellowed orders, clearing the decks of wounded, having broken rigging spliced, turning to look back at the quarterdeck and Sophie was by his side, clinging to his arm, her foolish fat face looking at him with a wondering excitement, a fond admiration, without so much as a quiver or a simper of fear.

"Oh, Foxy!" she said, hugging him. "My hero — Lud — how you made my heart beat."

He felt a shiver of disgust.

All he'd done was commit this tiny vessel to receive a broadside that should have blown her clean out of the water. The carpenter should have reported by now. The surgeon could be left until he had seen to the wounded. And where the hell was Commander Mortlock? Sophie was still hugging him and Lord Kintlesham was standing by her, beaming all over his seamed face.

Mortlock was lying on the quarterdeck. A piece of langrage had lacerated all one side of his face so that his eyeball showed clear, like a marble, glistening and veined.

Fox was forced to break Sophie's hold on him putting her fat arms aside. He saw Mortlock was carried below. He felt numb and shook himself roughly. The frigate was after them, creaming along, with all her sails pulling. *Raccoon,* he fancied, was just keeping ahead. If they snapped a spar now it would be all up with them. Those Frog gunners had played their usual trick and fired high and missed. They'd used grapeshot and language, and they hadn't hulled *Raccoon.* The carpenter reported no shot holes below the water line. Fox felt an evil glow of joy.

The chase continued through the rest of the afternoon. Surely, Fox thought, the frigate captain wouldn't chance coming this far north. He must know the British Fleet commanded all this area of the Mediterranean. Then the reason for this apparently reckless chase made him annoyed with himself for missing the obvious. Naples had fallen. The French were in command there now. Maybe a Fleet had slipped out of Toulon and was even now bearing down on Naples to attack, with fresh troops, Sicily and Palermo. Naples must have fallen; that could be the only explanation.

The frigate was keeping up with them. Fox felt that there was a growing gap; but it was a damnably small one.

Commander Mortlock had insisted on going to his own cabin and Lord Kintlesham, who had been quartered there, agreed. All his feelings for the commander had changed as soon as the man was wounded. Fox felt tiredness on him like a grey blanket, warm and fuzzy; he would have to go on all night alone now.

Sophie would have his cabin. He thought of that gross bulk in his cot and half-smiled, and then forgot her in fresh calculations as to their rate of progress. The wind held. If it died and the frigate held it — he refused to think of that.

A sudden shriek from forward made him look up sharply.

"Man overboard!"

The cry was repeated. A body thrashing in the water went sweeping past. Fox could see a head and a waving arm in the wake.

Midshipman Prentiss panted on to the quarterdeck.

"It's Grey, sir! He was on the fore tops'l yard —"

"Grey!" Fox didn't want, now, to know how it had happened. A man was in the water, they were drawing away from him farther and farther every second, and the French frigate was nearing them with inexorable mathematical logic. Grey. A useful lad. Probably a future admiral. Well, the idiot should not have slipped. What had he said? What Midshipman Lunt had said. So? Fox wondered, with a panic that came icily to denigrate him in his own estimation of himself, which was small enough in all conscience, that he was going soft in his old age. Just a snotty — did he measure anything in the balance that held a whole brig and her company in the other pan?

"By God," he said, aloud. "I won't lose Grey."

He looked forward, and his face was as ugly and vicious as any mythical demon-dragon. "Back the main top's'l! Lively now. Mr. Carker! Take the best boat's crew we have — and you've got exactly ten minutes!"

"Aye, aye, sir!" shouted Carker. Mr. Lassiter had the jollyboat over the side, the crew were tumbling in, swearing, the cox'n jumped in and then Carker, the master's mate. Fox watched stonily as the boat pulled away. *Raccoon* began to rock. He cocked an evil eye at Prentiss.

"I'll trouble you, Mr. Prentiss," he began, "to practise your signalling. It's a downright disgrace. Make some practice signals."

"Signals, sir?" Prentiss gaped.

"Signals, I said! Send: "Am in need of a cargo of women!" and, Mr. Prentiss, you need not enter the signals in the log."

"Aye, aye, sir." Prentiss went to the flag lockers, his face screwed into puzzlement.

A furious bellow reached Fox's ears. He saw Mortlock, his head bandaged and the white bandages dreadfully stained, bound on to the quarterdeck. The commander threw his hands high into the air, his lips worked and spittle ran down his chin.

"What are we hove to for, Mr. Fox?"

"Man overboard, sir."

Fox eyed the commander warily. The man was demented. Those bandages must be chafing his exposed eye and sending excruciating pains throughout his head.

"I don't give a damn a man's overboard! Don't you understand we're being chased? That frigate will smash us — smash us —" Mortlock's lumpy face contorted. He really began to foam now, spittle and froth from his lips.

"It's Midshipman Grey, sir —"

"I don't care if it's the Queen of Sheba!" Mortlock raged and ranted. No one dared approach him. He was, clearly dangerous. He turned to the quarterdeck rail. "Brace up that main tops'l! Get under way again! Jump to it, you mutinous dogs!"

There was great danger here. The man was still the captain of *Raccoon,* still giving orders. An enquiry would recognise that a captain was doing his duty, was a gallant officer if he continued in command even if wounded to death. And he was the son of a Lord; Fox was a nothing. Fox had to decide.

He went to the quarterdeck rail. The men were moving to the braces, looking confused.

"Belay that!" bawled Fox. "Keep her as she is."

Mortlock swung around as though struck. His face with its bloodstained bandages leered horribly on Fox. "Mr. Fox —" he started to say. "Mr. Fox —" Clearly, he could no longer remember what he had wanted to say.

A voice hailed.

"Here comes the jolly boat."

Fox roared. His left eye was completely blind now.

"Hoist her inboard. Brace up your yards!" He swung back to look aft. Through the noise of the jolly boat coming out of the water and the men clacking and Grey jumping down, wet and dripping on the deck, Fox heard the noises in his own head, the dread sounds of what his court-martial would pronounce, with the point of his sword turned towards him.

Then he saw the French frigate luff up. She fell off. She was giving up the chase. "Mr. Prentiss," he said, with the vicious unfriendly tone evident in his voice and manner. "You may leave off signalling now."

Grey was standing before him, smiling shamefacedly, yet full of an eager bubbling excitement.

"Thank you, sir. Thank you. I thought I was a goner then. Never thought you'd stop, what with a Frog in chase." He babbled on. Clearly his ducking had loosened his tongue. "And to signal like that, sir. Sheer inspiration! The Froggies must have thought Admiral Nelson and the whole Mediterranean Fleet were over the horizon. Magnificent!"

"Get below and change those clothes, Mr. Grey," said Fox. His eyes — both of them, although only one was working — starring with undisguised disapprobation on presumptuous Mr. Midshipman Grey. "I'll deal with you later."

And here was Sophie, hugging him, her fat arms around him chirruping and chattering, about how wonderful and marvellous he was, and a credit to the Navy and the country.

"We only picked up a boy who was stupid enough to fall into the sea," he said.

"You're too modest, Foxey," she chattered on. "When we reach Palermo, you and I will see a great deal of each other, Never you fear."

Fox shuddered. Her fat softness sickened him. He thought of the trim firm softness of Kitty. It could never turn out the way it did in your dreams.

During the rest of the passage as Mortlock raved in delirium and Sophie did what she could to nurse him, outraging Fox, who, like all navy men, considered it a man's prerogative to nurse the wounded, he kept the vessel functioning perfectly. She was clearly too deeply laden; lightened by a good half of her cargo of marble, she would have walked away from the frigate. That frigate would be sniffing around now, searching for the phantom fleet. Lord Kintlesham was beside himself at Fox's stratagem. Fox saw with his own cynical brand of realism that it would pay him to, as it were, "keep in", with the Kintlesham's ideas.

A noble lord with three or four seats in the House in his pocket was an asset of unimaginable price to a naval officer. Lord Kintlesham had been mightily impressed by George Abercrombie Fox. He was evidently perfectly under the impression that as soon as this cargo of his antiquities had been landed at Palermo Fox would return for another. He kept on praising Fox. Fox found it unnerving, sinister, frightening.

"And I think I'll have a word with Sir William. He might be able to have a word with Admiral Nelson. You know, my boy —" How Fox winced at that "My boy!" —"It doesn't do any harm to have a friend at court."

Fox knew that well enough. He looked at silly fat Sophie. She was the price. She had made that plain enough and her father had made equally plain his attitude. "If my Sophie wants something then I get it for her. I've more money than I know what to do with. I don't give a damn about your money, my boy — look at Nelson! Once you have your own ship you'll soon be able to claim a knighthood, and a title, too, given your aptitude for licking the Froggies! You'll be an Earl in no time!"

Fox thought about that. An Earl. With Sophie as his countess. What a fate! What a future! Then the memory of his family rose in his confused mind, of his mother, and his brothers and sisters. The pride they would feel would recompense him in some measure, and far more fruitfully, the comforts and luxuries he could give them. He could really provide for them if he was an Earl, flying his own flag, in command of a squadron or a fleet, an admiral, taking the lion's share of everyone's prize money. Prize Money; he could stand a life with silly fat Sophie for that.

He looked at her, simpering, her red cheeks burning under the Mediterranean sunshine, she was his Prize. She was the fat galleon he had towed into port.

At Palermo he saw to landing Lord Kintlesham's marble heads and torsos. On the following day Mortlock died. He was given all the rites of a naval funeral. The other men dead when the French frigate had blasted that broadside at them had been buried at sea, and the wounded were now taken ashore. Fox began to wonder about finding replacements.

He hadn't even kissed Sophie. The idea appalled him. She ventured to hold his hand in the drawing room of the house Lord Kintlesham had taken. She simpered at him, her secret making her bright blue eyes moist, her red lips pout even more.

"Foxey, dearest heart —" He swallowed. Everyone who ventured on the intimacy called him Foxey. Only his family, and Rupert Colburn, ever called him George, it seemed. "I'm not sure how it should be worded." She giggled, clasping his hand in her little sweaty palm. "Papa spoke to Sir William who happened to mention it to his wife and she must have been talking to Admiral Nelson. Now commander Mortlock is dead you are being confirmed in the command of *Raccoon.*" Fox jumped. Then he refused to think; but just listened. "Of course,

I don't understand it at all. But they cannot promote you to commander because you haven't done anything brave or heroic they know about."

Well, that figured. She went on to add that, of course, she knew how brave and heroic her dearest Foxey was. They'd be married as soon as they could; but she would have to languish for some time yet, the exigencies of the service being what they were. "But," she said finally, with a deep sigh that set all the upper portion of her bodice rolling like a three-decker in a gale, "But, dearest Foxey, I do love you. I don't mind that you aren't a peer of the realm. I love you for being my Foxey."

During the period that followed Fox was only too glad to be able to go to sea. There was a great deal to do for a brig at this time. Christmas came and went. The antiquities of Zamba languished there as the Kintleshams languished in Palermo.

Then, out of the blue, Fox received orders. By this time he had *Raccoon* in something like the condition he wanted her.

"Oh, Foxey, beloved!" wailed Sophie. "Where are they sending you now?"

George Abercrombie Fox said one word. "Acre."

THE END

Made in the USA
San Bernardino, CA
16 January 2017